PRINCIPLES
of
PREDICTION

PRINCIPLES
of
PREDICTION

Anushka Jasraj

cntxt

First published by Context, an imprint of Westland Publications Private Limited, in 2020

1st Floor, A Block, East Wing, Plot No. 40, SP Infocity, Dr MGR Salai, Perungudi, Kandanchavadi, Chennai 600096

Westland, the Westland logo, Context and the Context logo are trademarks of Westland Publications Private Limited, or its affiliates.

Copyright © Anushka Jasraj, 2020

ISBN: 9789389648713

10 9 8 7 6 5 4 3 2 1

Typeset by SÜRYA, New Delhi

Printed at Thomson Press (India) Ltd.

MIX
Paper
FSC FSC™ C010615

CONTENTS

DRAWING LESSONS

1

My husband has a mole on his left eyelid that looks like smudged kajal. I have a mole above my belly button. I'm told it's a sign of fertility, but this has proven untrue. A mole on or around the eyes could mean domestic trouble or bad luck with finances, my astrologer, Mr Nayar, informs me. He wants a photograph of my husband's mole, since my husband works all day and could not accompany me for this consultation.

The astrologer wants me to retrieve the photograph from home, but even this simple outing to Nayar's Destiny Bazaar – a ten-minute ride from my house, and five flights of stairs – has exhausted me. I ask him for a piece of paper and a pencil instead, and I draw a picture of my husband's eye from memory. I've been taking drawing lessons from a woman named Flora. She comes to my house on Mondays and Wednesdays, and for the past five weeks we have been drawing bowls of fruit: mangoes, apples, coconuts, lychees. Soon, I hope, she will teach me figure composition.

Nayar traces his finger along the drawing, as if the texture of the paper might reveal something. He wears large gold-plated rings on both thumbs and his fingernails have the sheen of a recent manicure. As he starts talking about the connection between the face and the planet Saturn, my eyes wander to a painting on the opposite wall. Shades of teal and turquoise in a diamond shape at the centre, surrounded by yellow and orange blotches, inside a mute bronze frame.

'All colours are hurt spectacles,' I think, and say aloud without intention.

Nayar looks at me, then looks around as though there might be an insect in the room. 'What's that?'

'Gertrude Stein,' I mumble. Suddenly the conversation feels like a crossword puzzle where the clues are wrongly numbered. I hand him five hundred rupees and leave without taking the notes he has written about rituals I need to perform.

2

I have a master's in English literature from St Xavier's College and mine is a love marriage, which means visiting astrologers is not something I have always done. In the past, I've sought answers in books. Poetry, Russian novels and the occasional self-help manual. Our mother once took my sister and me to a man who stared at my palm and told us we were all cursed. We rolled our eyes; a pair of disbelieving schoolgirls who took pride in our ability to recite the periodic table. If you asked me to trace the impulse that brought me to Nayar, I would draw a blank.

'Pascal's wager,' I tell my sister, when she expresses her disapproval. She calls every day at 4 p.m. and we talk for an hour, and then I spend an hour in the kitchen, supervising the maid as she prepares our dinner. Mustard leaves, spinach leaves and radish leaves, sautéed with garlic and green chillies. 'I can handle this,' she says in Marathi, 'go practise your drawing.' I feel like I've been dismissed, my housewifely presence rendered unnecessary.

3

It is Monday. I wait for Flora with anticipation. The rest of the day is blurred, boring and without texture. The Pomeranian, whom we have named Igor, announces Flora's arrival by barking before the doorbell rings. He stops barking when I open the door and sniffs around Flora's small feet as she takes off her blue chappals.

She carries a large sketchbook and a box of charcoal pencils in a backpack meant for schoolchildren. It looks out of place slung across her shoulder, next to her carefully braided silver hair, and even more so when she places it on the floor next to her, in this house bereft of children.

We sit next to each other at the dining table, and I tell her I want to try portraiture. She seems pleased that I am showing initiative. 'Something simple first,' she says. She sketches an oval on my sheet of paper and shows me the basic shape of a face. 'Try to draw me,' she says. 'Don't get stuck on any one part. Keep your hand loose. Don't look down at the page too much.'

We move our chairs so we are facing each other. She looks at me with a mixture of encouragement and acceptance. She is offering herself up to the brutality of my inexperienced hand. I start with the mouth: her lips are thin. There are wrinkles deepening around her eyes. I pause, and she asks to see the drawing.

'You've made me look young,' she laughs, and touches my cheek. 'Don't be afraid to draw my old age. Try shading. Move the pencil in the same direction, but apply more pressure.'

I want her to draw me, but it's an intimacy I will not allow myself. I am afraid of the feelings it might evoke. We end early because I am tired. She looks over the drawings and says, 'Your lines remind me of Kokoschka.'

Flora types the name into her phone and shows me portraits by Oskar Kokoschka, an Austrian expressionist. Our heads are almost touching as we look at the pictures together. I breathe in the scent of her talcum powder. Often, we take breaks during the lessons, and she shows me pictures of drawings by famous artists.

Before leaving, Flora asks to be paid. I bring out my chequebook and write out her name. 'Flora B-H-A-V-N-A-N-I. Sindhi?'

She nods.

'Flora is a Catholic name,' I say.

She shrugs, then smiles. 'I was born in Chembur only, back when it was a refugee camp in 1950. I've lived here since then.'

I ask whether she has any children.

'One daughter. Married a few years ago.' She doesn't elaborate, and something in her demeanour stiffens. For a moment I catch a glimpse of another Flora: a woman who has tried, and failed, at motherhood.

4

I'm thinking about Gertrude Stein again, and how Karun memorised lines from her books to impress me. He calls, and I don't answer the phone because I already know he won't be coming home for dinner. My phone trills to announce a text message: 'Why aren't you picking up? Getting a drink with co-workers. Will be late. Love.'

I met Karun at a party hosted by a mutual friend, who was intent on setting us up for reasons as yet unknown to me. The friend later claimed she had an intuition that Karun and I would make an *alchemical match*.

'What does that mean?' I once asked, suspecting we had been pushed together as a social experiment.

'Just, you know, I could tell something transformative would happen,' she said.

Karun was training to be an architect and I was a graduate student hoarding notebooks filled with bad poetry. He smoked, and I didn't like the smell of it. My perfume made him sneeze and I didn't understand his humour, which involved riddles and violent knock-knock jokes. The person I was back then – a stranger to myself now – agreed to a date, and then five more, before we slept together. What got to me was his attunement to the external world. Everything around us opened up when I was with him. He was always pointing out things: a strange-looking bird, a surreal street sign, a man selling kites and flutes, the beauty of a building I walked past every day. After a year of marriage, I realised Karun's outward-looking nature was also an evasion: we watched strangers while sipping filter coffee at outdoor cafés and imagined ourselves into their lives, but rarely spoke about our own. 'You never reveal anything about yourself,' I complained once.

'Revealing too much can be just as pathological as repression,' he said. 'Doesn't that cloud look like a kangaroo?'

5

It is five in the morning when Karun gets into bed. If I ask, he'll say, 'I came home at one, I was watching television in the living room.' I know this to be untrue because I was in the living room till 4 a.m., watching re-runs of the news.

A question I know the answer to is also a question harbouring an accusation. I don't ask where he was last night. Instead, I find myself being nicer to Karun at breakfast – placing a kiss on his neck, which he doesn't acknowledge. In this way, our marriage is two separate marriages. The one inside my head, filled with potential, and the one I confront in Karun's presence.

6

When my sister calls at our usual time, I explain to her that I'm in two marriages with one person.

'Why are you always so difficult, darling,' she says. 'I was just telling Baby about how you got into trouble for constantly reciting the national anthem when you were thirteen. They even sent you to the school nurse.'

'They sent me to the counsellor because I refused to answer annoying questions. I would recite the anthem instead, but I'm not sure why I chose that.'

'You're such an oddball.'

I change the topic and ask about her son, who attends a small liberal arts college in North America and was recently arrested for drug possession. She sounds tired. 'We found a better lawyer,' she says. 'But he might get deported.'

'It might be nice to have him back,' I say.

'I'm sure this makes you happy,' she sighs. 'I couldn't keep even one son in check.'

'You know that's not true, Tarini. I want you to be happy so I can feel unique in my suffering. Anyway, I had a strange dream the other night. I was speaking to a child over the telephone. It was an old rotary phone. The child was crying and wanted directions to my house because she was lost. I couldn't give her directions because she didn't know where she was. I kept asking her questions, but she wouldn't stop crying. It was very distressing.'

'Are you still considering a second round of IVF?'

'No, I don't know. Karun is worried about the expense. And please, I don't want to argue about your money again.'

Tarini doesn't push the matter or offer me the money. We are both too tired for our usual fights. She tells me about the new television show her husband has been making her watch. It's based on the myth of Hanuman, and all the Hindu gods have modern superpowers. 'Damn annoying. I think he wants to have a second child just so he can keep watching these cartoons. I have to go now,' she says. 'I'm making a casserole.'

I have always been envious of my sister's name, and never understood why my parents gave her the sweet, normal, Indian name while I was called Moira. 'It's from a book,' my mother had said when I asked.

'What book?'

'I don't know. A good book. Ask your father.'

'I don't remember,' my father said.

It made me furious. But now I know: Moira means destiny.

7

On Monday, Flora arrives earlier than usual and asks if I want to take a walk before we begin the lesson. It is thirty-five degrees and cloudless outside, but before I can respond, she confesses: 'Your husband called me yesterday because he's worried about you and he asked me to get you to go out. He said you've been more cheerful since we started the drawing class. He thinks I'm a good influence. I'm sorry. He asked me not to tell you. He's just concerned, but it felt so underhanded to not tell you that.'

My throat closes up. I feel hurt. For a moment my thoughts drift, and I place a hand on my neck and ask her if it's too warm. 'Should I turn up the fan?' I say.

'Are you upset with me?' she asks, with unexpected tenderness. 'It is a very hot day. We don't have to walk. Look.' She grabs my wrist and presses my hand to her left breast, then brings it to her right breast. 'They feel different,' she states. I am too stunned to respond.

'They feel different,' I say, parroting her words and her tone.

She tells me about her breast cancer and how she had a full mastectomy of her left breast. 'At my age it didn't seem necessary to get a reconstruction. But sometimes you almost miss being viewed as a sexual object. Why am I telling you all this? I know you and your husband have been trying for a child. I know what it's like to feel betrayed by your body.'

'You don't know my situation,' I say, surprised by the coldness in my voice.

Flora doesn't say anything for a while. She arranges the drawing materials on the table. Then she talks about colour theory and aura. 'Let the object tell you what colour it wants to be,' she says. We work in silence, making watercolour paintings of a small copper mug.

8

According to Goethe, 'Objects are often seen by sick persons in variegated colours. Boyle relates an instance of a lady, who, after a fall by which an eye was bruised, saw all objects, but especially white objects, glittering in colours, even to an intolerable degree.'

9

At dinner, Karun asks about my day, but I don't mention Flora, or the fact that I know he spoke with her. He tells me about a new client who calls for a meeting every few days because she keeps changing her mind about her plans for the house. 'One day she wants all wood and bamboo, the next day she watches some movie and wants marble-topped everything. So another late night tomorrow.'

'That's fine,' I say. 'Tomorrow I am thinking of going out for dinner with the girls. Tina wants to try the new Chinese place.'

My husband's mole glows magenta. 'Very good,' he says, with the authority of a doctor examining an X-ray.

The girls are my friends from college: Tina, Urmila and Yogita. I haven't spoken to any of them in months and I have no intention of doing so. Tina is pregnant with her second child, Urmila's first daughter started school recently, and with Yogita's children I've lost count.

They appear in my dreams that night, perhaps because I've told this lie and made them my unwitting accomplices. Tina keeps telling me her bladder wants to burst while the other two are squeezing my breasts. They think I would have a good career as a wet nurse. They leave and Flora arrives. She undresses because she has agreed to let me draw her, but I am overcome with lust and ask if I can kiss her. I explore her body with my hands and tell her I want to paint her in orange and gold. I kiss her neck and lick the scar on the left side of her torso.

'Amazon women cut off their breasts so they can be better warriors,' she tells me, and suddenly I am afraid: not of her, but of me and what I feel.

10

I write a note to Flora. I spend an hour trying to get the wording right. Am I unable to continue the lessons or am I simply no longer in need of them? Do I send her my warmest wishes or my sincerest regards? In the end, I write that I am terminating the lessons because I would like to invest more time in other parts of my life. I send the maid to Flora's house to deliver the note, along with the money I owe her, and an additional thousand rupees. After she leaves, I berate myself for choosing the most blatant lie.

I try reading a book about how nutrition affects thyroid and fertility, but my mind wanders and I play a game of *Would You Rather*. I already know all the answers. Be betrayed by my own body or my husband's body? Lose an appendage or lose my marriage? Suffer or tell the truth about my desires? Die at the age of fifty or never experience childbirth?

The maid returns with the money. 'Flora ma'am said no need,' she tells me, in a combination of broken English and Marathi. She hands me the money, along with a book that Flora has sent for me. *Doctrine of Colours* by Goethe. I pore over it, searching for a note, an underlined sentence, a dog-eared page, but there is no sign of a message from her.

When my sister calls in the evening, I do not mention any of this.

11

The days move slowly with nothing to look forward to. I visit the astrologer, but he has nothing new to tell me. The future looks the same as it did two weeks ago. I finish reading Flora's book and call her one evening, hoping she will forgive me.

'What is there to forgive,' she says in a neutral tone, though I don't believe her.

'Can we start classes next week?'

'Why not,' she says.

It's June and the rain clouds have arrived. I ask if she wants to take a walk after our class.

'Why not,' she repeats.

I read to her from the book. A passage from a section about colours and their shadows.

'Yes,' she says. 'We could even go to the Hanging Gardens and collect flowers.'

I close my eyes, and the image of her from my dream appears. Goethe calls these extraordinary affections of the retina. I search for something to say that would cement the shift in our relationship. 'I missed you,' I tell her, and hear a smile in her voice when she says, 'See you next week.'

CIRCUS

My great-grandmother could dislocate her left eyeball from its socket. She was part of a travelling circus show for a week, but she fell in love with my great-grandfather, who worked at a pharmacy in South Bombay. She claimed she had the power of the 'vision', though this was not part of her circus act. The 'vision' is the protagonist of numerous family stories. In one story, women bring my great-grandmother offerings of food and drink and in return she informs them who is sleeping with whose husband. It is a running joke that women in my family have the 'vision' but are blind to the philandering of their own spouse.

My great-grandmother died in 1979 and I was born the same year. I never met her. On my thirteenth birthday, my mother gave me an eyeball preserved in a glass jar. The iris is grey, like clouds announcing a thunderstorm. I have kept it all these years. I also inherited her 'vision'. It tells me I will meet my true love when I join the Kohinoor Circus. I wonder whether Heron will come to see me perform. My act will be called Daring Draupadi. My real name is Sita.

In order to explore my ancestral roots, I am reading a book about circus life. The author is a Japanese man who fell in love with a trapeze artist named Mala, and followed the circus around India for five years. That is two years longer than I have been married, and I am already planning my escape. I practise contorting my body every morning after my husband leaves. When the circus reaches Bombay for the summer, I will join.

I found the book at a used bookstore; someone has drawn moustaches on all the animals and the binding is damaged, but the photographs have maintained their sheen. The Japanese man writes about a skeletal old woman who does not eat. At each performance, she walks around the ring and the audience watches as the circus master offers her a glass of water. It sounds mundane, but it is one of the most dramatic moments in the show, because any day now, the woman is expected to collapse. At night, the author watches the woman, expecting to find her sneaking food from a pocket hidden in the voluminous folds of her sari. Instead, he discovers that she sleeps heavily and snores like a steam engine.

Under my bed, I keep a large glass aquarium filled with formaldehyde, in which Billy the cat is preserved. My husband and I adopted her two years ago, and she died last month. On my honeymoon in New York, I saw a work of art by Damien Hirst: a shark preserved in a giant aquarium-like contraption. I spoke to a woman at the information desk, and she told me about the various struggles involved in the process of keeping the dead shark in the gallery. I had wanted to keep the cat because a soul exists in the body and disperses as dust once the body is burned. Billy still has her soul.

I cannot take Billy with me when I join the circus, but I take her from the glass box and leave her corpse in the oven. It will be a surprise for my husband. He never looks under the bed, but he will find her in the oven.

Every morning I take five multi-vitamins and one tablet that stops ovulation so I do not become pregnant. My husband's name rhymes with heron, and he does not know I am on birth control. He is forgetful. He eats almonds with his breakfast and fish curry for lunch to improve his memory. 'It's strange,' I tell him, 'that fish are such forgetful beings but we eat them to remember better.'

I call him Heron because it is disrespectful to speak his name. When I am alone I say his name to myself: *Kiran.* I am expected to cook all his meals and have sex with him weekly. The unexpected consequence of such an arrangement: a desire to know and be known. The closest Heron comes to expressing tenderness is when he says, 'You don't eat enough.' On Sundays he watches my favourite TV show with me, without complaining. There is a dissonance between his lack of affection and the intimacy of our shared life.

On Wednesdays, I fast. The doctor says it is unhealthy, but I tell him I cannot take any medicine on Wednesday. I take a double dose on Thursday. 'This is nonsense behaviour,' the doctor says. When my mother falls ill, I fast for an entire week, and consider joining the circus. I understand the skeletal woman's strength. My doctor tells me anorexia is addictive because the body releases hormones that stimulate hunger and simultaneously energise the mind.

My mother likes to remind me that I was always a nuisance, and sometimes, I blame myself for her fragility. All her aches and pains began with me, with complications during her pregnancy. These days she spends her time knitting and sends me woollen garments in the mail, even though the weather is hot and I never have any use for them.

She took me to the circus when I was five. The first act was a magic show, and we had to leave early because I would not stop crying after the magician vanished two doves into his hat. I was slow to learn object permanence.

Heron runs a furniture store, which he inherited from his father when we got married. Ten years ago, Heron's father advertised modern furniture and fixtures. Now it is a vintage store selling the same things. I have difficulty believing things can exist when they are not in my possession. Does it also work the other way around?

When I'm alone, I wonder whether I exist. On days when Heron is at the store, I invite my downstairs neighbour, Saila, to drink tea and watch a movie. Sitting next to me, sometimes her hair brushes against my face and I feel comforted. She is beautiful, her breasts perfectly proportioned. I fall in love with beautiful women because beauty is symmetrical and contempt is the only asymmetrical facial expression. I imagine my husband would love me if I were more like them, but I'm looking for ways to make him forget me. My breasts are not quite symmetrical. I stop wearing a bra and allow my nail-paint to chip. I use unscented body wash because I want to smell like a stray cat in summer.

I practise saying goodbye to Heron in front of the mirror but it is not easy after three years together, so I decide I will write a note instead. In the first draft, I list fifteen things that are wrong with our marriage. I stop at fifteen because I am reminded so strongly of my misery that I cry for approximately two hours. My husband calls to say he will be late because the business dinner is a seven-course meal. On the radio, a woman sings about crossing the sea to learn a language in which she can make sense to her beloved.

I rewrite the goodbye note, but this time I try sounding cheerful. These years have been the best years, I write. I steal lines from the Japanese man who followed the circus. 'Never before has such a spectacle been created, and this death marks the end of a silver age of circus-masters.' I keep this incomplete note hidden in my jewellery box. There is so much more I need to say before departing. Usually my mother has dominion over my guilt, but I've made promises to my husband, which I must now break.

My true love is Rajan the Lion-tamer; I know because I have the 'vision'. When the circus arrives, I read the reviews in the *Bombay Times* and discover that my true love is a hijra, though he prefers the male pronoun.

I dream about Rajan and realise he is the perfect creature – if we are all searching for the half that will complete us, then he is already perfect – both man and woman. But then I wonder how the perfect creature can be man and woman, when there is infinite love for Saila in my small heart. She senses my moods from the rhythm of my footsteps, which she hears from her apartment below. When I collapse from sadness, she hears the sound of my body hitting the floor and comes upstairs to find me. I wish she would ask me to stay. I can predict many things, but cannot always predict what will make me happy.

Before leaving to join the circus, I must retrieve the glass jar with my great-grandmother's eye. It is in a corner of the closet behind a deflated beach ball, a box of cracked wine glasses, three pairs of rain boots and a Styrofoam angel. On my last night as a domestic woman, I sleep with the jar held close to me. In the morning, I find it has fallen to the floor and cracked open. There is a vague chemical smell in the room. My great-grandfather had worked in a pharmacy and must have smelled like this every night when he got home to my great-grandmother. I take this to be a good sign. I clean the floor with paper towels, wrap the eyeball in tinfoil and pack a suitcase.

I write the final note. It says: *These last few years have been the best years. I have loved you, and I will remember you. I am leaving because in my heart there is growing –* The note remains incomplete because I am searching the dictionary for the right word to explain the emptiness inside me which is also a kind of nourishment. Language is a rigged carnival game where the hoops are too small to fit around any of the prizes. Friendship. Desire. Love. Loneliness. None of these words can explain what I experience. I decide to stay another day, until I finish the goodbye note.

Saila comes over and we watch a Kung Fu movie without subtitles. She kisses me on the cheek when I tell her I will leave once I finish writing the note. Her lips are dry and her breath smells of ginger.

'I'll help you,' she says, and we spend an hour flipping through the dictionary and trying out obscure words we haven't heard before. Astraphobia. Ecophobia. Frabjuous. Stultiloquence. Sigilism. Twaddle. Tosh. Zyxt. Zaum.

'How about despondency,' Saila says.

'I am hopeful. My true love is Rajan the Lion-tamer.'

'He's a hijra,' Saila says. Her tone is devoid of judgement, but she puts down the dictionary. The game is over.

I call my bedridden mother for help, but I do not tell her my true love is a hijra. I merely say, 'I think there is someone else for me. I can join the circus. I have been practising and I can twist my limbs into a jalebi-shape. I'll send you a picture. Check your email.'

Mother says, 'Don't make mistakes.' I'm not sure whether she means the same mistakes she made or mistakes in general, because the latter is mostly impossible, and my mother is always placing impossible demands on me, like the time she asked why I wasn't on the tenth grade honours list when I was still in the ninth grade.

'Was I a mistake,' I say, trying to lighten the tone of our conversation.

'Sleeping with that man was a mistake, but you are a blessing,' she says. 'Apart from the cysts I developed while breast-feeding and the occasional incontinence from having given birth. I still pee myself a little when I sneeze.'

I do not know anything about my father except that my mother met him at a neighbourhood Diwali party and they had sex behind a water tank on the roof of a nearby building, after which she never saw him again. Mother was twenty-two, and raised me alone, with monetary help from my grandfather. Her friends avoided her once she became noticeably pregnant.

'It was dark,' she says, whenever I ask about my father. 'I do not think I would recognise him if I saw him.'

Every time I see a middle-aged man with dark curls, I imagine he is my father. These men are generally dressed in shabby, un-ironed clothes, suggesting bachelorhood. They are not successful men, but they have jobs and spend their lives in a state of distractedness that prevents them from confronting the emptiness of their existence. I fantasise about finding my father and bringing new meaning to his life.

I leave on a Monday. The note is still incomplete, but some things take too long and must be forgotten in order to move forward. I have been fasting and the hunger is making my bones weak. When I twist myself, everything creaks like a house swollen with water after a flood. I do not cry; tears are not a sign of weakness but a form of blindness.

I am sure the lion-tamer does not have children, and I doubt he is married. What woman would allow her partner to insert his head into the mouth of a wild cat every day?

The circus is stationed at the cricket maidan. I arrive two hours before the first show. The heat and nerves make me sweat. I sneak into the main tent, which I hear someone refer to as the 'thambu'. Inside it is a small planet. There are five hundred seats surrounding the ring and the fabric walls are shimmery polyester. The performers are at the back of the tent, but their voices carry loudly to the outermost seats where I am sitting.

Nothing has prepared me for the melancholy feeling that accompanies me while watching this absurd show in an auditorium devoid of other spectators. An old man in a clown costume juggles eggs. The acrobats, all blue sequins and feathers, are stretching in one corner. Rajan the Lion-tamer feeds unidentifiable meat to the lions. I approach the ring, and the clown notices me.

'What are you doing here,' he says. 'Audience is not allowed until six.'

'I want to audition,' I announce, loud enough so everyone can hear.

The circus master walks over to me and says, 'No. I know your type. Go back to your family before things get worse.'

I cry because there is nothing else to be done. I can go home, destroy the note before my husband gets back from work, ask Saila to forgive me and have everything revert to its original state. The circus is like an accidental comet and I can only return to my orbit. A deep sadness lingers in me as I watch each act rehearse simultaneously in their corner of the ring. I realise that I will never be so limber. I will never fly.

The lion-tamer sits down beside me. His beard is unkempt, like iron filings collected around a magnet. I feel myself pulled toward him, I rest my head on his shoulder. He seems startled, but allows it. 'It's not easy,' he tells me, 'being envied in a freakish manner. The audience leaves and goes back to their lives, but this is it for us.'

'I can wash your clothes and cook for you. I make the best idli-sambar.'

'Don't waste your tears on this silliness. Go.'

'I am taking a vow of celibacy.'

Rajan laughs. 'Why, child?'

'For you.'

He goes quiet when he sees that I am serious. 'All of us live in small tents just behind here. Mostly, people share. Two or three in one tent. I am alone. No one wants to share with me. Do you understand?'

I nod, but my eyes follow the trail of scars along his arm, the bump on his shoulder, the spidery birthmark on his neck. Already I have decided to follow him back to his tent.

How is it that the entire world is not in love with him, I wonder.

There is a break before the show. The lions are led into cages, which are then locked and wheeled out by Rajan and the old clown. I stay out of their sight, but follow them by the sound of creaking wheels. The cages are stationed a few feet from the circle of tents. Rajan goes into one of the tents. I move closer and hear him talking, but I cannot make out the words. I do not realise that he can see my silhouette through the thin cloth walls. He emerges and yells at me. 'What are you doing here?'

He raises a hand to his forehead, as if shielding his eyes from the sun or wiping away sweat. His defensive posture makes him seem more fearful than angry or annoyed. The cowhide whip, shiny from disuse, is still in his left hand. I want this creature to tame me, but first I must break into his life.

The Japanese man writes that an animal is indifferent when you are outside the cage looking in, but he transforms once you enter his abode. I hold Rajan's gaze without flinching. He looks at the ground for a moment, as if preparing to attack, but I ram my shoulder into him, and even though I am not strong, he is too stunned to stop me.

Inside, there is a sleeping bag on the floor and a small cot on which an emaciated old woman sleeps.

Rajan sleeps on the floor and relinquishes the sleeping bag to me. The old woman, I recognise as the woman from the Japanese book. She is small enough that Rajan hides her in his bedding when the circus travels. She speaks Tamil, a language I do not understand. Rajan translates between us. 'Her name is Kamala. She is ancient. She probably knew Mr Barnum personally. Founder of Barnum and Bailey circus,' Rajan says. Sometimes she says things that are meant for me, but he refuses to translate.

I am not allowed to perform. In fact, I must remain hidden if I want to travel with Rajan. He agrees to take me along because he feels pity, or perhaps I've grown on him. Rajan has become habituated to me, just like my husband. He will find a way to sneak me onto the circus train when they depart for Jaipur next month.

Rajan tells me about the two lions: 'We had four more, but we could not afford all that horse meat and had to auction them. These two are Leo and Castor. They are special because they come from a lineage of lions bred by Carl Hagenbeck in the nineteenth century. My ancestors on my grandmother's side were hunters in Bengal and they supplied Hagenbeck with elephants and tigers. He gave my great-great-grandfather a gift – a lion cub from a Belgian menagerie, two years old and trained like a dog. Have you ever been to Europe?'

'No, I haven't.'

'One day I will perform there. The International Circus agent is coming to the show this week. We see him once a year. This time I have some new tricks.'

Pinned to a wall and fluttering slightly in the wind is a sheet of paper listing names and cause of death:

Trieste caught a bad cold.
Bolivar was attacked by a jealous lover.
Titus in a fire.
Atir drank a barrel of liquor and had a seizure.
Old Betty – psychosis.
Darling, June, Jenkins and Felix of old age.
Zora ran away.

'Are these people you performed with?'
'Lions,' he says. 'Bolivar was the only tiger.'

At night Rajan touches me through the sleeping bag, but never directly. An animal is a different beast once you enter his cage. He places his palm against my palm, layers of cotton and polyester between us. 'We are born alone and we die alone,' he says, quoting some poet, 'but strange that we are built to feel such loneliness.'

'Like fish in water, thirsting for oxygen,' I murmur.

'I would like to be an immortal jellyfish,' he says.

The old woman croaks from her cot but Rajan does not translate for me.

When I was a child, my mother told me bedtime stories that always featured talking animals and had a moral. My favourite one was about a crocodile eating a monkey's heart. I often thought about a lion's heart. To have a lion's heart is to be brave, but what about the lion whose heart you have?

Two days before the agent is expected to attend the show, Rajan takes me to rehearsals. The lions are not present. Chet, a light brown horse, trots around the arena while a Great Dane stands on a pedestal in the centre. 'This was last performed in 1873, at Hagenbeck's travelling menagerie. He trained a lion to ride a horse. First, you need to allow the horse to get used to having another animal's weight on his back. I have been training Chet to perform with the dog on his back.'

On Rajan's command, the dog runs, leaps onto Chet, and balances on the horse's back like a prima ballerina: all four legs drawn together and neck stretched out. I applaud, but no one else at the rehearsals looks impressed.

'Today we will try it with Castor for the first time,' Rajan says. A special saddle is strapped onto Chet's back to prevent Castor's claws from digging into his skin. Rajan opens the gate and Castor saunters down the steps that have been placed at the cage door. The trapeze artists, usually dismissive of the rest of the circus crew, become attentive. Even the Great Dane seems on edge. Castor is made to stand in the centre. Rajan walks alongside Chet and around the ring. Once. Twice. The third time, he whistles: loud and sharp. Castor stands on his hind legs, Rajan whistles again, and Castor bounds over to Chet and leaps onto his back. Chet is startled by this new weight and pauses for a moment, as if deciding whether he should bolt. Rajan pulls Chet's reins and murmurs in that secret language formed between animals and their caretakers. The horse calms down and continues on the circular path.

There is a painting by George Stubbs in which a lion is attacking a horse. The painting depicts that moment when the lion has leapt onto the horse and sunk its claws into the flesh. It could be a scene of passionate love as much as it is a scene of vicious attack. The lion has not yet drawn blood.

Castor falls ill the night before the agent is expected to attend the show. He is restless in his cage, walking back and forth in the 8"10' space. Leo snarls at him. I can hear

Castor moving in his cage, and then Rajan brings him into our tent. He has placed a muzzle around Castor's mouth. 'Have you ever cuddled with something that could eat you?' Rajan asks. The lion shifts its head from side to side as if trying to speak. 'He's harmless,' Rajan says, and unhooks the muzzle. Castor throws up a puddle of bile. It smells like milk that has been boiled for too long.

Most days, while the show is on, I stay in the tent with the old woman and tell her stories from my life, even though we do not speak the same languages. Under the old woman's cot is a small metal box containing a map of Belgium from the 1850s, a black-and-white photograph of P. T. Barnum, a miniature porcelain lion, a yellowed copy of Hagenbeck's *Beasts and Men*, a lion's canine tooth, and a blue paper flower.

I attend the show today because I am worried. Mr Magri, the agent from the International Circus, is seated in the front row. Mr Magri looks like his name. His moustache stands delicately above his lips, as if it is about to fall off his face. In the circus gossip circuit there are rumours that he is a descendent of Count Primo Magri, the famous Italian dwarf. He is of average height, though.

We do not usually have a full house, but word has got around about the special performance. Saila, or someone who looks like her, is in the audience. I wonder whether she'll be proud of me, or perhaps she blames me for the sad look in my husband's eyes when they pass each other on the stairs of the building. It hurts to imagine my absence unfelt and a new woman in my place, so I banish this thought.

After the show, Mr Magri joins the performers in the dining tent. He walks over to speak to Rajan. 'That was a neat trick,' he says. There is a long pause. Magri realises we are waiting for him to continue. 'Oh,' he says. 'I'm afraid – it's just that – audiences these days are looking for something with more heart. More of a story. This act is a bit terrifying. I must go say hello to the escape artist before he gets away. It was very good to meet you, Rajan.'

Magri leaves, and Rajan holds my hand. This is the first time we have touched. Later, I will pray for forgiveness because I am happy, like a starving animal grateful for a drop of milk.

NOTES FROM THE RUINS

1

'In 1906, my great-grandfather was steering the ship. Fifty tons of gold, fifty bales of cotton, three Bengal tigers and two hundred passengers. The queen had asked for the tigers. My great-grandmother warned him. She said, "The waters have been whispering about you." He said, "I'm not scared of a few fish." Then, in '72, the gold was recovered near here. My great-grandfather was identified by his teeth. The cats' bones were never found. You know what they say: ten lives and smart as yogis.'

The landlord took pleasure in telling this story to each new tenant of Wanli Mahal: a five-storey building resembling the wreckage for which it was named. Dahlia, whom the landlord had cornered in the compound, was unable to contain her amusement. The landlord looked hurt. 'I'm sorry, I'm sorry,' she said. 'I haven't laughed in a long time. I don't like wild cats. My mother passed away recently. It had nothing to do with cats though. I just don't like them.'

The landlord coughed and coughed. 'Excuse me,' he said, and walked away.

Dahlia lied. Her mother was alive and healthy as a kitten with all fifteen organs intact. It was her father who had passed away – years ago – and her mother had recently embarked on a pilgrimage of the northern cities. Dahlia had been sent to stay with her cousin, Laldeep, who insisted on being called Lilya.

Back at Lilya's flat, which was now her place as well, Dahlia panicked when she noticed a slender man lounging on the living-room sofa. His grubby shirt suggested recent homelessness.

She had read about this in the *Newcomer's Guide to Mumbai* when she arrived from Jaipur. They were called palathis, and usually inhabited vacated building complexes. The guidebook had foregone a proper procedure for ridding one's living space of these squatters, simply stating: *they are often delirious creatures and should be avoided.* Dahlia stood paralysed, until Lilya emerged from her bedroom.

'This is Prakash. He lives here sometimes. Don't look so shocked. We're not doing it or anything. But please don't go and tell your sister, or the entire khaandan will start talking about it.'

Prakash, who had been watching Dahlia as if she were a baroque chair, introduced himself. 'Struggling actor,' he said, putting the word struggling in finger quotes. He taught workshops for eight-year-olds on weekdays, and spent weekends rehearsing with an experimental theatre group that called themselves Mumblesnore. 'We met through Mumblesnore,' Lilya said. 'Dahlia's a historian. She just moved here from Jaipur.'

'I'm not a historian. I study historical ruins. Elphinstone College.'

2

Prakash offered to show Dahlia the Gateway of India, and Dahlia thought he was just being hospitable; after all, he did live in her flat, rent-free. When he bought her a balloon from a young man selling them on the street across from the Taj Mahal hotel, she decided it was something other than kindness.

Prakash pointed at the Taj and said, 'The architect planned it so the front would face the sea. But they misread the plans and built it backwards.'

'Even your city's architecture is unwelcoming.'

'My city,' Prakash repeated, as if testing an incantation. 'You live here too now.'

'Maybe,' Dahlia said. It was later that she noticed how Bombay was a place riddled with unbelonging; like cartoon illustrations in a novel of grave seriousness. The small child playing a rhythm on a plastic drum in the middle of the morning rush at Dadar Station, Armani-clad men lined up for glasses of falooda at Shalimar, taxi cabs with interiors that shimmered like wedding gowns.

The Newcomer's Guide said, *Mumbai has many beauties to be appreciated. These are also places where you are most likely to get robbed.*

3

On their second date, which Prakash insisted was their first, he took her to Juhu beach and they wrote things in the sand with small pieces of driftwood. 'It was exactly like in that picture with Govinda and Madhuri,' she said to her sister, who lived in Dubai.

'You need to stop watching those duffer movies.'

'He wrote me a poem. I don't understand what it means. Listen. "I live on your lips." Next line. "Like the silence of the ocean." Next line. "Curled up in an empty conch." Next line. "Waiting for the wind."'

'Stay away from these types,' Maggi said. 'He won't pay your bills.'

'I have to go. I heard a click. I think Lilya is listening on the other line. Have you heard from Mum?'

'No. She sent a postcard. Hold on. Here it is. It says: "The unreal never is. The real never is not." That's from the Gita, I think.'

'How cryptic. She and Prakash would get along.'

'You're one to talk.'

After the requisite sand-sculpting and feet-wetting, when even the flute-seller had retired, Prakash had led Dahlia to a part of the beach usually reserved for teenage couples or prostitutes. He slipped his hand under her skirt, fumbling like someone looking for a light switch in the dark. The men she'd dated in college usually introduced her to their mothers before taking her to the cinema, where they proceeded to graze elbows or hold hands. She smiled politely. This must be what the guidebook meant when it said, *One must adapt to local customs and the speed of city-life. Try not to look surprised in order to blend in.* His presence is irresistible, Dahlia thought, but his absence un-notable. An object bringing luck to the bearer. Five letters.

4

On date number four (Dahlia kept count), Prakash had cooked dinner. Dal and basmati rice. Saltless but comforting, Dahlia decided. He claimed to know three jokes. 'I'll tell you one. What did the apsara say to the man?'

Dahlia shook her head.

'Leave your shoes on the shore.'

Dahlia smiled, unsure where the joke lay, feeling bad for the barefoot man, gill-less and beguiled.

'It's important to have jokes memorised,' Prakash said. 'Entertaining people get eaten last.'

Wrong, she thought, and sprinkled salt into her bowl when Prakash wasn't looking. It's not the jester who gets eaten last.

'I think we should get a cat,' she said.

Prakash slow-zoomed his arm through the air and lightly punched her shoulder, giggling like a schoolboy. 'This is what I love about you,' he said.

'That which is a beggary, if measured. Four letters,' Dahlia said.

They didn't have sex that night because Dahlia was menstruating. 'Not even a blowjob?' Prakash had asked. 'Just kidding,' he added, too quickly.

5

Dahlia started attending Prakash's rehearsals, occasionally helping out with lighting effects and props. Mumblesnore met on Sunday evenings at the Bubbles auditorium, which was part of a nursery school owned by the director's cousin. All the furniture was child-sized.

'I don't understand,' she said.

'It's an allegorical exploration of bestiality,' Prakash said.

The actors crawled around the miniature stage on all fours, snarling like lions in heat.

6

Lilya sometimes made breakfast for Dahlia, and brought her small gifts: a book about the Mughal Empire, a plastic flower that bobbed from side to side, a bottle of rose oil, a mug with 'Know Thyself!' printed across in large blue letters. What do these gifts mean, Dahlia wondered.

Prakash left for work before Dahlia woke up. He wrote post-it notes, which Dahlia held on to. These too were gifts whose meaning she tried to unlace:

Won't be home for dinner.

Out. Love, P.

Morning! You snore like a train.

Kisses & Waffles.

We are like trees. XO.

U rock.

The three of them ate dinner together on weekdays, and Dahlia felt like the child of too-young parents; a possible accident, something they were obliged to love. Lilya offered to lend Dahlia her clothes and Prakash asked if she had found anything in the ruins. 'These kurtas are comfortable, but thank you for offering,' Dahlia countered.

'I'm not an archaeologist, I study discoveries that have already been made.'

After dinner, Prakash and Lilya always cleaned up together, refusing Dahlia's help. 'You are the guest,' Lilya insisted.

'Gender roles,' Prakash said vaguely, without forming a full sentence.

7

'You don't like to talk, that's fine. You could at least make some sound. It's like having sex with a cadaver. I can hear crickets,' she said one night, having been introduced to the tongue-loosening qualities of red wine. *It is not unusual for men and women to interact freely in public while under the influence of intoxicants.*

Prakash made an effort to be more expressive during sex. As Dahlia straddled him, doing most of the work as usual, he called out: Laila. This brought things to a stop.

'What did you say?'

'It's this play I'm writing. It's as if Majnun has inhabited my head. Laila was his other half. You are my Laila.'

'What happens to Laila and Majnun?'

'In the original version, they can't be together, and Majnun goes mad and kills himself. But I'm re-writing it. Majnun won't go mad; he'll just pine briefly.'

'Oh,' Dahlia said. She thought Prakash's voice sounded more high-pitched than usual when he spoke about his play. She reached for the iPod on her bedside table. Asha Bhosle sang through the small silver speakers in Hindi: *What thing is the heart? Take my life if you will.* 'It's okay if you don't like talking. We can play music to drown out the crickets.' Prakash shrugged. The room was too dark for either to see the other's face.

'Isn't it strange,' she said, 'how we're constantly shedding dead cells. Thousands and thousands, every hour. These will all have fallen off in a few years. We'll be the same people, in new skins, but we won't have noticed.'

'Keratin,' Prakash said.

'What?'

'That's what we're made of. On the surface. Keratin.'

'You smell like grapefruit,' Dahlia said.

'Do I? I borrow Lilya's shampoo sometimes.'

8

At Red Box – date twelve – the waiters looked reluctant to approach the table at which Dahlia and Prakash were seated. Can they see something, she wondered. The way she had seen it on Prakash's skin; on his arms and legs, but mostly in his desperation to please her, and in his puppy dog eyes. The restaurant walls were lined with mirrors, to give the illusion of endless space. The reflections moved like synchronised dancers whenever she shifted in her chair. She looked at Prakash, wanting to squish his worm-like eyebrows.

She thought about the time when Prakash and Lilya had locked themselves in Lilya's room. 'We're rehearsing,' Prakash had said.

'Slow processor,' Maggi once said, when Dahlia punched her in response to an insult, twenty-four hours after the fact.

Dahlia wondered what her mother had meant. *The unreal never is. The real never is not.* Or was it the other way around?

'What was the second joke,' Dahlia asked.

'The second joke?'

'You said you know three jokes. You've told me one.'

'A baby fish is swimming in circles on a warm July evening, and a grandpa fish waves out to him and says, "Aren't the waters lovely today?" The baby fish says, "What the hell is water?"'

'Seven letters. Least likely to get it.'

Prakash looked befuddled.

A waiter said, 'Would you like a tour of the tomato garden? We grow our own.'

'No,' Dahlia said. 'I'll just have the soup.'

That night, Dahlia dreamed of a beach replete with shiny glass pebbles. 'They used to be shards from broken bottles,' a phantom stranger said. The waves crash against the shore and wear down the sharp edges. 'That's the opposite of what happens with people,' Dahlia said. 'The sea is just the night, watered down,' said the phantom.

'You were talking in your sleep,' Prakash told Dahlia.

'Maybe I'm still asleep,' she said, and pinched him.

'Ouch,' Prakash said.

'They found a ship stranded at Juhu beach. It was in yesterday's paper. It was supposed to be taken to Alang to be scrapped, but the storm brought it to the shore, and now they can't move it.'

'I heard about that.'

9

Dahlia spread a rumour that Lilya's milky skin was the result of nightly rituals involving a pumice stone and Pond's Fair & Lovely. The girls who were part of Mumblesnore's backstage crew laughed about this, spitefully, then went out and bought tubes of the lotion for their own use.

She watched Lilya and Prakash rehearsing. They crawled, along with the other actors, their animal noises beginning to resemble the braying of plump frogs. Dahlia noticed the largeness of Lilya's breasts relative to her own. Too bad she's not rich, she thought. There were things she could say about those melon breasts, if Lilya were rich.

10

A professor from Delhi University visited Elphinstone College. Dr Ramnathan specialises in places that are no longer remembered, the posters claimed.

'The city of Prashta had a gift economy, and they had no concept of marriage. The men lived in groups while the women lived alone with their children and occasionally paid visits to the houses of the men. It was up to the woman to choose her mate, and naturally, the women were generally polyamorous. We cannot say whether or not they had any concept of love, though there have been findings of drawings that suggest they believed the afterlife to be a time of eternal monogamy, and perhaps they saw life as an extended expedition during which we are meant to find our mate for the next world. A theory that can be neither proved nor disproved.

'The Prashtians worshipped Indra, who is considered to be the Hindu counterpart to Zeus. Kama, the god of carnal love, is said to be Indra's slave within Prashtian mythology, suggesting that the qualities they valued included the ability to overcome primal desires – a philosophy that might seem contradictory at first, in light of their dating customs or lack thereof. And as we can see from these images, Kama was depicted as having a phallic weapon—'

Someone in the audience whistled, and the lecturer blushed. He was young. Dahlia saw him in the cafeteria after the talk, sitting alone and drinking a Coke. She handed him a paper straw and said, 'Those things are covered in rat's piss. I enjoyed your lecture. I was wondering—'

'You want me to sign a copy of my book?'

'No, I didn't know you had a book. I was hoping you could tell me more about the theory of—'

'It's all in my book. *Civilisations Besieged: A Chronicle of Forgetfulness*. You can buy it across the street. I can sign a copy for you.'

Dahlia walked away with no intention of returning.

'Thanks for the straw,' he said, as she was leaving.

11

'What are you going to do,' Maggi said over the phone.

'About what?'

'Dahl. Wake up. He's using you. It's been three months. You need to tell him to move his caboose out of there.'

'Don't call me that. I'm not some side dish. Have you heard from Mum?'

'Yes, wait. This one has a picture of a baby haathi. It says: "Hope is the penalty for despair"'.

'That woman is hilarious.'

'She didn't mean to, you know—'

'To withdraw; often in the face of danger or encroachment. Seven letters.'

'I hate it when you talk like that.'

12

Rehearsals for *Majnun's Life* began, and suddenly everything seemed like a scene from Prakash's play; a series of borrowed motions. They were just miming the words. Dahlia was assigned the task of lighting director. The contact sheet stated: *Lightning director – Dahlia S.*

There were no other misprints. The part of Majnun would be played by Prakash, and Lilya would play Laila. 'Such similar sounding names,' the director said, as if that had clinched his decision.

13

Majnun: I slept with Laila.

Tulip: What?

M: I don't love her.

T: How did it happen?

M: I don't want to talk about it.

T: Why did you tell me?

M: I don't know. I'm sorry.

T: Why did you tell me?

M: I love you.

T: You expect me to forgive you?

M: I love you.

T: How—

M: I don't want to talk about it.

T: Get out. I want you to leave.

M: For now, or for good?

T: Just go.

M: I can't live without you.

T: Then don't.

M: It didn't mean anything.

T: I don't want to hear it.

(Curtain)

Majnun is alone. He holds a blue tulip.

M: Life is like a circus that's left town, and you're left behind, burned by the world's most beautiful beard on a lady the size of a bear. The posters cast shadows, but soon the wind takes even that away, like a leaf folding and unfolding. You wish you had the trapeze artist's graceful nose or at least his ability to resist the forces of gravity. Madness is said to be the breakdown of negotiations between selves. I will eat my tulip, representative of eating my actions.

Dahlia read this while lying next to Prakash in bed. She kept her face still because he was watching her. *Try not to look surprised in order to blend in.* 'I like it,' she said. 'Red tulips mean love. Yellow tulips mean love beyond hope. But there's no such thing as a pure blue tulip.'

'And dahlias?'

'Stars of the devil,' she said, without meaning it. The same tone as when she'd said, 'My mother passed away.'

14

Opening night was a semi-success. 'The auditorium is half full,' the director said in his pep talk. Dahlia climbed a ladder and positioned herself behind the key light. She watched Majnun and Laila devour each other's faces before parting, and wondered whether it counted as polygamy if a man was sleeping with one woman in reality and the other in pretense. Maybe that's why Bollywood actors marry Bollywood actresses. The thought caused despair.

Prakash, or Majnun, was about to deliver his monologue. Dahlia slipped a colour gel into place and flooded the light. Prakash glowed red. Dahlia wondered how different things would be if she were named for some other flower; a more exotic variety like orchid or hyacinth. She increased the intensity of the spotlight and watched Prakash break into a sweat. Dahlia had never seen him naked; they had sex at night, in the dark, as if underwater. His thin shirt was soaked by the time he got to the finale, and Dahlia could see through to his murky skin. She wondered if his outfit was fireproof.

Lightning director, she said to herself, and smiled as the audience gasped. Connection of low resistance, established unintentionally. Twelve letters. Thick plumes of smoke left a layer of ash on her arms and face. No one had listened to her when she suggested the exposed wires might be a fire hazard. The spotlight had short-circuited.

The third joke, Prakash had told her before going onstage: 'What did the goldfish say to the apsara?'

'What?'

'Nothing. He forgot what he wanted to say.'

It was a riddle, and as with all things related to apsaras, she didn't think it was funny.

The smoke cleared, and Majnun emerged looking charred but charming, like something accidental. The play did not have a second night. 'This is inappropriate for children,' the school principal said, even though there were no children in attendance. Dahlia rubbed the black dust on her arms, till it flaked off like bits of dry skin.

Backstage, Prakash said, 'That did not end the way I'd expected.'

'Denouement – no – you haven't told me how many letters,' Dahlia said.

'I'm not blaming you, but I won't be home tonight. Drinks with the boys.'

15

Lilya's diary:

Poor thing poor poor thing. She loves him quite irrationally. Mother abandoned her. No other family here either. She can't leave him, and he won't leave. She thinks she's some tragic heroine from his play. I'm much better off, not loving. I tried to broach the subject with her, talk some sense into her. I even dropped hints that he and I were lovers. She seems to think love is like those ugly pictures in her textbooks – holding a hidden beauty whose appreciation requires an imaginative leap.

VENUS IN RETROGRADE

'I teach horoscope, palm-reading, face-reading and kundli-matching. Extra charge if you want to learn how to draw star-charts,' Akash announces. 'We are like doctors who comfort hypochondriacs, but our job is telling the Johnny things that will make him feel enlightened. Here is an example. Spin in circles like a ceiling fan while reciting your wish to the walls of the room. A private room is ideal for conducting the ritual; the more windows the better. Paint your nails with Maybelline Peppy Pink and apply turmeric underneath your eyes. If you spot a cat on your way to work, follow it. Never worry about being late.' Akash looks at Laxmi as he reads from a small notebook. He's reading to the class, but wants the words to resonate with her.

The clients are referred to as Johnny – Akash prefers this to 'customer' or 'purchaser'. He thinks it is romantic, the way buxom women in Hollywood films refer to men who pay them for sex as John.

Makhija, who owns a paan-shop, wants to know what hypochondriac means. 'Hypochondriac is someone who enjoys visiting the doctor,' says Akash, who once took his wife to see Dr Mehta and is familiar with medical terminology.

'What nonsense,' Makhija says.

'I've heard Ayurveda is just placebo,' Laxmi says. She pronounces the C in placebo like a hard K.

Akash never gives his clients bad news unless there's a remedy. When he looks at the lines on Laxmi's forehead, he knows he can never tell her the truth of what he sees: an affair with a madman will cause her grief. Could I be the man in her future, he wonders, then brushes the thought aside. These premonitions are never specific enough to be useful.

There are no chairs. The students sit cross-legged, forming a semi-circle around Akash on the concrete floor. They meet in Akash's flat, in a tenement building near Dharavi, on Wednesday evenings. The five students fill the small room, where Akash also receives customers. He teaches them the Art of Occult. On the walls are various diagrams of obscure constellations, and maps of the body annotated with corresponding emotional characteristics. According to the markings, the left side of the chest carries general sadness, and the central region holds the pain caused by betrayals.

'We can discuss all your concerns at the end,' Akash says to Laxmi.

He first met Laxmi outside Jalsa, Amitabh Bachchan's bungalow, in Juhu. Every Sunday, hundreds of people gather there at 6 p.m. in the hope of seeing the Bollywood superstar. Bachchan emerges from the gates any time between 6 and 8 p.m., and waves at the waiting crowd.

Those nearest the gate were rewarded with a handshake. Some Sundays he didn't appear at all. Nonetheless, people station themselves there with chairs and picnic baskets, playing cards and guitars.

Akash went to Jalsa every Sunday and offered palm readings, while Laxmi often went and gave shoulder massages to the waiting women for a small fee. They noticed each other and decided to combine their services. Special discount for thirty-minute massage accompanied by a palm reading to predict what time Bachchanji would be spotted. Eventually, Laxmi asked to learn more about astrology.

Akash rewinds a cassette in the tape recorder. 'This customer came to me last week,' he tells the class. The voice in the recording is scratchy, but this is a side-effect of the technology. Akash remembers the young man as having a crisp voice, like someone in a street play. After fast-forwarding through the greetings, Akash presses play.

'I have developed an obsession with all forms of wishing paraphernalia and superstitions. Always careful with fallen eyelashes (even those belonging to other people); always watching the night sky for shooting stars (and sometimes airplanes); always looking for four-leaf clovers (even between the pages of used books). I keep a journal. At present I have noted down two hundred and thirty-six ways in which to wish for one thing. Some of them are my own invention.

'Underwater while holding your breath and pretending to be drowning in an ancient well. Every time you see an ugly baby. When it rains, with your tongue sticking out to catch the droplets; each raindrop its own separate wish. Upon extinguishing a candle – birthday or otherwise. While eating an entire red rose; petals, stem, leaf and thorn. Each time you encounter the word in a book or a newspaper article: wished, wishing, wishful, wishy-washy. Most importantly: never ever reveal the wish itself. But you already know that – yes, you have studied these things.

'My brother is a pragmatist, but you and I both know all kinds of things are possible. You haven't met my brother. His name is Vikas. It is easy to confuse us, but he is the smart one. He is in his first year of architecture college. He wants to design tall buildings. He was always – academically – the golden child and a stellar draftsman.

'I used to have a recurring dream in which my father sprouted black feathers. They grew slowly and obscured every part of his body. "It is a painful process," he explained, before flying away. A few months after these dreams began, my father abandoned us, and my mother moved us to a small apartment on the outskirts of the city. That was when your sister returned to her village. We did not have enough money.

'Mother worked the night shift as a nurse at an old people's home. Our house was littered – or decorated, depending on how you saw it – with belongings of the deceased. Framed pictures of someone else's loved ones. A purple divan cover with gold-trim and the letters ND embroidered into a corner. A tree built from umbrella spines. Books from a time when I was barely an idea in my mother's mind: *The Ocean of Stories*, *Panchatantra*, *Lucknow's Lilith*, *Collected Poems of Tulsidas*. I kept a Sanskrit *Kama Sutra* hidden among my clothes. I cannot read the script, but I found the illustrations informative.

'There were other dreams which I wrote into stories, and I once won a handwriting competition at school. I was in the fifth standard. My story was displayed on the class bulletin board for an entire week. That was many years ago; now I am twenty-four, working as a filing clerk at an accountancy firm, with no time to recall what occurs within the confines of my subconscious during sleep.

'Why am I telling you all this? You only need to look at the lines on my palms, and you'll know everything. Thing is, some details are impossibly specific, and I don't want you to get the wrong impression. Who was it that said, "Life is a process of breaking up"? Or was it "Love is a process of breaking apart"?

'It wasn't my father's disappearance but Ayah's leaving that was my first real experience of loss. Your sister was like a mother to me. People say that, and one suspects it is an exaggeration – something sweet to say about someone we miss – but I drank the milk from her breasts when I was born. She was hired for that purpose, and then she stayed to take care of me. It was Ayah who finally gave me a name. I have studied this in junior college; all these brainy theories about childhood experiences and the role they play in defining our character.

'"Everything is a love story," Ayah would tell me while I sat on the kitchen counter, watching her grind cinnamon or peel away layers of red onion. She made two of everything: one large bowl of spicy potatoes for everyone else, and a small bowl without mirchi for my baby palate.

'You don't mind that I'm telling you all this? Thing is, there's a girl. Her name is Simran.

'When I first saw her, she reminded me of a deer; fragile and likely to be frightened by sudden movements. I couldn't approach her – I am not a shy person in general, but she made speech seem impossible. It's not that she's beautiful. It's a constellation of the little things about her that make me want to journey outside of myself. The delicacy of her wrists and the silver-blue bangles shimmering against her skin; the mole on her chin, and the light fuzz because she bleaches her facial hair; the way she stirs her coffee after every two sips; how her left ear sticks out more than the right ear.

'I once asked Ayah, "Why do stars twinkle?" She said, "It's because they're made only of light; unlike the planets, which are solid rock formations." Simran is more star than planet – and I mean this in a manner of speaking. She still lives in Malad. The one-seven-two stops outside her building. I always worried she would vanish, since light is exhaustible. You understand. You and I, we are planets.

'We've met before – when I was eight years old, and Ayah brought me to your flat. The two of you spoke in Bengali, and you spoke too fast for me to comprehend any of the words. I have been wondering what you meant that day, when you took my hand and said: "You are a tricky one. Heart stronger than head. Prone to somnambulism. Wife will need to chain you to the bed. There's something dark in the future."

'You were about to tell me something about the future darkness for which I was destined, but Ayah made you stop because I was frightened. Wait. I'm not ready to hear what you are about to say. I have more to explain before we get to that.

'Simran doesn't believe in things that seem to exist outside the natural order. She denies everything science cannot explain. You know what she once said? "Horoscopes are absurd. One in twelve people will have a romantic adventure this weekend. How is that possible? And they can't be any less vague. They can't say: a piano will fall on your head today, so better watch out. There just aren't enough pianos in the world for that to happen. And anyway – a romantic adventure assumes two people and Taurus is incompatible with Taurus, which means two in twelve people will have adventures this weekend. The world is too repressed for that to happen."

'And then, as a joke, she read me her horoscope. She is Aquarius; a volatile personality and quick to burn. The horoscope said, "Trust is a gift you should not be giving away easily."

'I've arrived at this part of the story too quickly. I need to explain. I have a friend whom I visit on Sunday evenings. She calls herself Payal, but I assume this is merely a professional name. We have a working relationship. I can give you her number; she offers a reasonable price. Hundred for a handjob; five hundred for normal; thousand for the entire night. Unfortunately, she won't put anything in her mouth. Women don't understand about these matters, but you know how it is; the body craves a certain kind of contact.

'One day I helped Simran with some work at the office, after that we went for chai, and so on and so on. We became inseparable. Everyone else thought we were going steady before either of us had realised. Thing is, I had never been in a serious relationship; I had only been in a working relationship with a professional girlfriend. I never had trouble with the ladies. I mean, do you see these teeth? White like in a Colgate advertisement. I have solid abs; nicely defined. It's just that non-professional women are too much hassle.

'When you fall in love, you like the hassle; that is what happened with Simran. We were going around for a few months, but nothing; not even a kiss. My brother, who wants to design tall buildings, told me: "There are rules and rituals in regular relationships. You'll need to stop frequenting prostitutes. Buy her flowers. Orchids. Gardenias. Potted plants are even better. Except cactuses. Never ever buy a girl a cactus. Tell her something about yourself that seems personal, but not so personal that she knows you too soon."

'So I bought her a small eucalyptus plant, and I told her about my special ability. I asked her, "Do you believe in clairvoyance?" She said, "I believe in self-fulfilling prophecies."

'She laughed, but I still don't know what was funny. This is always the case with non-believers. They think magical things are silly; they think I'm a Suppandi. We fought that day.

'Later, she apologised. She said, "I'm asexual." I was confused at first; I thought it meant she was built like a

Barbie doll. I asked my brother – he said it means she has no sexual urges. It is almost like a Barbie doll. So you can see why I needed to continue visiting professionals. I could not leave Simran either; you can tell from my palm. I have a very strong heart-line. It means I love with great passion; that much I know. I have a question. I'm getting to it. Do you charge per question or by the hour?

'The problem was, Simran started suspecting that I was seeing another woman. Women have special built-in antennae designed for sensing infidelity. She said, "How come you never try to have sex with me?" She said, "You never even try to initiate anything. Either I'm not attractive enough or you're getting it somewhere else. Who is she?"

'Love made me reckless, and I told Simran I was seeing a ghost-woman.

'"What does that even mean," she said. "I see dead people."

'"You see them too?"

'"I'm mocking you."

'"Since you don't believe," I told her, "you should have zero problem."

'She seemed displeased but she said, "As long as it's just sex."

'The difference between an imagined experience and a lived experience diminishes with the distance of time. I feigned a ghost, and eventually the haunting became real. I left taps running, doors unhinged, unusual objects appeared (although the flat was strange enough with my mother's habit of hoarding), and I once hired someone to throw a stone through my window when Simran was spending the night.

'Yes – she would often stay at my flat, and we would cuddle like two paralysed hedgehogs. Do you know hedgehogs are drawn to each other for warmth, and then they hurt each other unintentionally because of their prickly spines, and then they separate, and then they miss each other. The whole process repeats. I think the stupidity of the hedgehog is his optimism. With Simran, I was like a paralysed hedgehog; I could not separate.

'But I'm getting to the matter regarding which I require your help. Do you really charge by the hour? I can pay half now and half later.

'The ghost-woman I invented started appearing in my dreams. She is a young Madhuri Dixit. Madhuri said, "You need to choose." In the dream, I was in a mithai shop, and I needed to choose what I wanted to eat; but what she really meant was I need to decide between Simran and Ghost-Madhuri. By now, it is possible, you have guessed what I sometimes wish.

'I chose Simran, but Madhuri keeps appearing in my dreams and sometimes, during the day, she walks around with ghungroos tied to her feet. Jangle jangle; all day. I can't see her, but the noise is distracting. Everywhere smells of jasmine. You must tell me how to – what is the word – exorcise the ghost. It could be my only chance to win back Simran's love.'

When the recording ends, Laxmi raises her hand before Akash can speak. 'I don't understand,' she says, 'Madhuri is not dead. How can she be a ghost?'

'That is beside the point,' Akash says. 'Any other questions?'

On weekdays, Laxmi works at Ladies Beauty Salon, where she trims and waxes and straightens. She has long hair; so long that in Akash's daydreams, when they have sex, it falls onto his face and obscures his vision of her peach-like breasts. Everyone calls her Lux – 'like Lux soap,' she says, making Akash sneeze (it is a nervous reflex).

'What are the main differences between face-reading and palm-reading,' Lux asks. She is trusting, her pen poised to note down whatever sugar-pill answer Akash offers. He imagines undressing her, though she refuses to appear wholly naked to his imagination; always masked by that long, wavy hair. It is an awkward, unnatural waviness; perhaps she braids her hair during the workday. No one should be allowed to leave such long tresses untamed. Akash thinks he would prefer Laxmi's hair in braids. He would wrap them around his hands like the reins of a racing horse.

Dolly, Akash's wife, suffers from a seasickness of the soul, even while her body is land-locked. She returned to Bengal to live with her mother but Akash remains bound to Dolly by the yellow thread he tied around her neck on their wedding day. He feels guilty for wondering whether Lux's breasts have the softness of ripe peaches and what it would be like to bite them. He decides to phone Dolly later.

Lux is looking at him with devotion. 'The difference,' Akash says, 'is a matter of performance. In hand-reading you are gentle and indirect.' He grabs Laxmi's hand with a clinician's sense of propriety and traces his finger along the vertical line cutting her palm in half. 'With face-reading,' he says – letting go of her hand and staring into her face with glazed intensity – 'you must make eye-to-eye contact.'

Akash assigns homework: 'What would you tell the young Johnny from the recording? Write one page.'

Makhija says, 'One page foolscap or half-foolscap?'

'One page of your notebook.'

Akash eats his dinner alone before calling Dolly, because he knows she will ask.

'Did you eat?'

'Yes. Rice and dal and onion with salt and lime. How are you?'

'I had satpadi roti and gatte ki sabji. Mummy cooked, special for me.'

'Come back na,' Akash says, as he always does. In these conversations with Dolly, he is truly prescient; he already knows she will say, 'I can't. Not yet.'

There is silence, and Akash's ear feels hot. His cellphone – an old Nokia model from another decade – is starting to overheat.

People come to him because he makes them feel understood. Strangers tell their secrets with such ease, he thinks. 'This line represents the heart. It is crooked, which means you are always travelling in the wrong direction,' he says, and they spill onto him like an overfull bottle. Everything about the woman they've pined for each day, or their fears of never being loved with passion, and things they hadn't thought until they sat down with Akash and he pointed out the path of a line on their palm.

Secrets told between strangers travel like soap bubbles; the words breathed rather than spoken, wobbly and reflecting light, making their way across the air from speaker to listener, and leaving behind an unnoticeable residue on those occasions when they make the distance without breaking. But Dolly is no stranger.

'Okay, I have to go sleep soon,' she says, and her voice sounds so small that Akash thinks she is speaking to someone sitting next to her, but then she hangs up the phone.

Akash dials Ayah, but she doesn't answer the phone. Another trick – of habit, not memory – for Ayah has been dead for two years.

Akash remembers everything Ayah taught him: how to make people believe in magic; how to make their sorrows bearable; how to make money by drawing maps of non-existent stars. He had been her protégé, years ago, when he first arrived in Bombay and spent nights at train stations or on bus-stop benches. She would be proud if she saw him today, he decides.

The following Wednesday, Akash asks long-haired Laxmi to read her response to the assignment. She reads. Her voice is enthralling and sonorous.

'On the first full moon of the new year, you must wrap yourself in a white tablecloth and swim in the lake. Both things at the same time. Be more generous with your money starting today. Rumi has said, "He whose love is lost loves longest." Find out where this woman lives and sing outside her window. Pray that she is not a lesbo. You can judge the depth of her love depending on whether she throws chappals at you or gets a restraining order. Wear a helmet.'

The class applauds. 'Waah waah,' Makhija says, nodding his head. The other students seem impressed by Laxmi's impeccable grammar. 'I took some help from parlour customers,' Laxmi says.

Akash says, 'It could use some tweaking. Often, in such a situation, you don't want to make any promises. Give the client some hibiscus-scented agarbattis and ask for his birth date. Draw on a piece of paper. Try to seem knowledgeable.'

'What did you say to him,' Laxmi asks. 'Did it work?'

'Sometimes you offer humanitarian advice. I've read the same textbooks as Dr Mehta. I passed the board exams. I know how these things are, so I told him to become an honest man. Stop visiting prostitutes, I told him. He took it the wrong way, and he left without paying me, but I predict that he will take my suggestion.'

Later that night, Akash performs a cleansing ritual. He destroys two hundred spools of cassette tape recordings and tears out the used pages from his notebook. He has learned that uncertainty is the only escape from despair and refuses to keep an archive of his predictions.

FELINE

Typically, I would never take on a case like this, but I was feeling sympathetic because my cat had just died, and you know how death softens people. The cat's name was Boccaccio, and with no one else to take care of, I had a lot of free time. The woman who approached me was named Anna. She pronounced it like she was Russian, but she was from Michigan; she had moved to Texas for library school. I figured the job would be a good distraction from my sadness: tail her ex-boyfriend-Jeff and find out whom he was dating and whether he loved her. I didn't want to get into it with Anna – her eyes looked red and puffy like she'd been crying a lot. But, like, who can say whether two people are actually in love or if it's just the dopamine pulsing through their bodies from all the fucking?

I prefer cats to people because boundaries are simple with cats. They stick to their corners of the house and approach gently when they require their belly to be scratched. With clients, I like to imagine a glass wall in front of me, as though I'm a cashier at the bank.

'Where does this get you,' I asked Anna in my gentle voice. The hostage-negotiator voice I used with Boccaccio when he got his teeth into a pair of stockings from the laundry hamper. I learned to use this voice after a client flipped out at me over the phone. I could hear something shatter in the background as she yelled, 'What do you mean where does it get me? Where does anything get me? I'm paying you to make my life easier.' She wanted me to find a replacement for an antique teapot belonging to her mother-in-law. Also, I work in one of those shared office spaces, so I have to keep my voice down.

I still ask the question, despite the teapot lady, and not because I expect anyone to have a real answer. I just don't want them to feel too optimistic. I like for them to know that there isn't a moment of epiphany once the case is solved, the object found. Nothing changes, and you still feel dejected, if not worse.

Anna looked confused. She tried telling me about their relationship and why it fell apart.

I said, 'I don't want to know.' My speciality is tracking down stolen objects: family heirlooms, antique furniture, paintings, jewellery, that type of stuff. People come in and they try to turn me into their therapist by telling stories about their sentimental attachment to their great-grandfather's gold-plated watch. I tell them their feelings are irrelevant.

I'm aware some people take pleasure in asking intrusive questions and learning everything there is to know about another person. But really, that's just like detective work, and I find it tiresome. There's no solution, no pay-off. A trail of clues leading nowhere. No matter how much evidence you collect, people still betray you, or they become strangers. Might as well not dig in the first place.

I'd underestimated Anna. She seemed to read my mind, and said, 'Losing him wasn't the difficult part. It's the destabilising knowledge that I loved him with my entire being, but the person I loved no longer exists. He's a stranger to me. And it's not like I want vindication. I'm not that optimistic. I need to know who he is now.'

I nodded and told her we needed to get into the important details. She gave me his address and a set of keys to his apartment. He lived in Allendale, a short drive from my office in South Austin. 'I don't need the keys,' I said.

'Throw them away. I can't bring myself to discard them. I don't know how.' I should have thrown those keys into the trash right then, but I come from a family of collectors. Things always find their use, my grandma used to say.

Anna had wavy, dark hair that she'd tied back in a ponytail. Her face showed no trace of make-up. I don't get involved with clients, but I could appreciate the beauty of her small nose. She fumbled with a blue backpack, brought out a money purse, and handed me five twenty-dollar bills. 'I'm not sure I can afford more than a few hours of your time,' she said. 'I'm a graduate student. I teach freshman composition.'

'That's okay,' I said, thinking about how Boccaccio's eyes matched the colour of Anna's boots. 'This is enough for a day's work. I should have all the information by the weekend's end. I'll tail him tomorrow and have my person snoop around his social media accounts. We don't need your passwords. Just permission to hack your account.'

'Oh. Sure. Jeff doesn't post much online. That's why I'm here.'

'Everyone leaves a digital trace these days. Maybe he has a Fitbit or something?'

'That's right, he does use one of those.'

'We'll find a way in. Totally legal too.'

'Great.' She stood up, and paused. 'I just need to feel like I'm doing something,' she said, then left.

I got started immediately, since there wasn't anything else to do. The pile of folders on my desk is for the benefit of the graphic designer in the neighbouring cubicle, who thinks I always look relaxed. She keeps a happy-lamp on her desk, which is meant to imitate natural light, so you don't get depressed from being indoors all day. 'We are living post-sunlight,' she informed me, which seemed like an odd thing to say. Maybe I misheard.

I called Eugene, and within a few hours he'd emailed me a fifty-megabyte portable format document with screenshots of Jeff's Instagram posts, including posts other people had tagged him in, and his Fitbit data. The last few pages contained line graphs with cartoon pandas. Some were smiling, some frowning, crying or blushing. According to the data, Jeff had significantly more frowning pandas during the months of his relationship with Anna. These days, most of his pandas were grinning.

Eating breakfast tacos, two-stepping, hiking the green belt, feeding turtles, kayaking, reading Victorian literature. These were Jeff's favourite activities to chronicle on social media. I wondered whether I had a responsibility to tell Anna that Jeff seemed happier without her.

Based on the photographs and the accompanying time stamps, I calculated that he would leave home around

6 p.m. and drive to a nearby bar to watch football and drink beer.

I parked my grey Subaru across from the entrance to his apartment complex and waited with my headlights on. It was November and the sun was setting. On the radio, California was on fire.

My mother had taught me how to hide in plain sight. I learned to blend in even as the only brown kid with an accent at my middle school in Connecticut. We moved there when I was twelve, and my mother said: 'Speak only when necessary. Stay away from boys taller than you.'

The weird, quiet kid whom no one remembers; that was me. Still, there's no childhood trauma I can point to, nothing to help some kinds of people make sense of who I am. A heart of stone, though you wouldn't know it from looking at me. I wear long skirts and peasant tops. I grow my hair long. I don't like being penetrated, I don't get attached.

I tailed Jeff without being noticed and waited in the parking lot, but grew bored after a while. It isn't like me to follow men into bars, but Jeff seemed harmless enough. They were playing Edith Piaf, and the place wasn't crowded. I started enjoying myself, and ordered a Lonestar even though I wanted a gin and tonic. A neon sign glittered above the bartender: Bullhorn Saloon. I chose a booth with a view of the table where Jeff sat alone, nursing a hard apple cider. 'Gluten-free,' I typed into the word document on my android phone. Even though it wasn't significant information.

For fifteen minutes Jeff appeared mesmerised by the glow of his phone. His thumb scrolled and occasionally paused to tap-tap on the screen in an almost sensual movement. After a while, he glanced around the room, then stood up. He left his jacket on the chair and headed towards the door leading to the back patio. I knew I would have to go out there and smoke with him if I wanted to get any worthwhile information for Anna.

I'd quit smoking a few years ago because Boccaccio didn't like the smell on me. He would hide under the bed until I'd taken a shower. Apart from that, he wouldn't leave me alone. Followed me around the house, splayed himself across my desk or on the kitchen table at dinnertime, purring for attention. He even stood outside the bathroom door when I shaved my legs or took a dump.

The porch was warmer than I'd expected because they had those outdoor heaters. I asked Jeff for a cigarette, but he didn't look up from his phone. I stepped closer, to get him to notice me.

'Could I bum one,' I asked.

He nodded and handed me the pack of American Spirits. 'You'll have to stand to my left,' he said. 'I'm deaf. Can only hear from this side.' He pointed at the translucent blue device coiled around his left ear.

I shifted to his left and asked for a light. When I spoke, he looked at my mouth, which made me self-conscious, like someone on the verge of being kissed. He leaned over and lit the cigarette held between my lips with a small orange lighter.

'I've been stood up,' he said.

I made a sympathetic face, or what I hoped was a sympathetic face, by furrowing my brows.

'It's this girl I matched with on Tinder. We've been texting for two weeks, and tonight would have been our first date. I thought we were really getting along, you know. I thought we had an emotional connection. But there's something unreal about virtual communication that seems to make it so easy to ghost someone.'

'Ghost someone?'

'Vanish on them. Like block them on Facebook, stop replying to text messages. In a way, you're dead to each other. But the vanisher's absence haunts like a ghost.' He smiled and said, 'How old are you anyway?'

'People actually went on dates back when I was a teenager.'

The music playing through the outdoor speakers rose in volume. 'Hold on,' he said, and adjusted a setting on his hearing aid. He lit another cigarette.

'What do you do,' he asked.

'I'm a shamus.'

'Like a healer?'

'A private dick. I forgot you're all of twenty-five. We don't speak the same language.'

'Okay then, Seamus. How'd you guess my age?'

I realised I'd gotten sloppy and needed to stay in control of the conversation. Anna had told me Jeff's age, his height, weight and zodiac sign. Aquarius.

'Probably from the way you dress. I've never heard of Depeche Mode,' I said, pointing at his salmon-pink t-shirt.

'What is it you do? Are you some kind of struggling poet?'

'Close enough. I'm in grad school. Medieval literature, like Chaucer and Milton and hey, are you crying?' He grabbed three napkins from a nearby table and handed them to me. I blew my nose and laughed.

'I'm having a strange week,' I said.

'You're funny.' He moved closer to me and said, 'It's very obvious that I could kiss you right now, but I won't.'

A fantasy of being fucked by him entered my mind. He smelled of frankincense, like the candles I'd burned in my adolescence while experimenting with pagan rituals. I tried to remember what my meditation coach had taught me, and allowed the thought to linger without obsessing over it. 'Like watching birds land and depart from a tree branch,' Coach had said. There's another meditation I learned from a book by Eve Sedgwick, where you imagine what someone would have been like if they were your mother. It brings a feeling of tenderness, but that didn't work either. So I told myself Jeff was a proxy for Anna, and by that logic I wasn't betraying our contract by sleeping with him.

We ended up at his place, with me driving my car behind his, pretending to follow even though I knew the way. We kissed on his bed, and he pulled off my skirt and panties and went down on me. I didn't want to arrive at the moment when he would try to enter me. I stopped him and said, 'I know Anna.'

'What? How do you know her?'

I told him the truth and started crying again, but really bawling this time. 'I'm no Humphrey Bogart,' I said. 'I help people track down stolen stuff from eBay. Not even the dark web or anything. Sometimes I just help them find replicas to replace lost or broken objects.'

He remained quiet. From the living room, I heard the sounds of someone crying on TV. I laughed, and Jeff raised an eyebrow. 'I think your roommate is watching *The Bachelorette*. Did you watch the last season? Can you believe Rachel picked the chiropractor from Florida? Where do you think rejected bachelors go in those limousines? Are they taken directly to the airport or to a nearby hotel?'

'Don't change the subject. Who are you, really? What proof do you have that Anna paid you to stalk me?' He reached for my purse and emptied its contents onto the bed. His house keys fell out. They were still on the key ring Anna had handed me. A small pepper spray and a plastic ballerina figurine along with two small keys.

'Why do you have these,' he said with a steadiness of voice that terrified me more than if he'd yelled.

I debated whether to grab them from his hand, in case he tried to pepper spray me. But then he might think I was trying to attack him. I chose instead to cover my eyes with my palms and said, 'I'm so sorry. I wasn't going to use them. Anna gave me those keys.'

'Anna stole my keys?' he said.

'No, you gave her a duplicate set.'

'No. I thought I'd lost them. Anna stole my keys. Unless you're lying. How do I know Anna gave you these?'

'I have a voicemail from her.' I picked up my phone and played him the message Anna had left.

A map of Appalachia hung on the wall facing the bed. My eyes wandered to the objects around the room while

Jeff held my phone to his ear and listened to Anna's message. There were no ghosts of ex-girlfriends lingering here. No feminine trinkets or 'Best Boyfriend' paraphernalia. No photographs of Anna or any other woman. Not even an ambiguous picture of a cousin, so someone might say: 'Oh, is that your significant other?' There were framed prints. Nature imagery mostly, and one of a lizard crawling out from a smoky chimney. Even the pillows were firm, so your head didn't leave a dent in the morning. I wanted to fling open the drawers to find where the messy parts of his past resided, but he watched me taking in the room and grimaced.

I tried to remain still, but I felt my stomach start to growl. Ever since Boccaccio died, I've had the runs. The graphic designer had told me a story about a woman who experienced daily, uncontrollable vomiting until she told her husband she wanted a divorce. 'By then,' the graphic designer said, 'the husband was so repulsed by the sounds of her retching that he didn't even mind. He agreed. It was very amicable, the entire thing.' When I asked what that had to do with my diarrhea, she said, 'Maybe there's something you're trying to purge too.'

This is Anna. I found your number on your website. I hope I'm not calling at a bad time. Umm. I was hoping to avail of your services to get some information on a friend. An ex-boyfriend, actually. I guess it doesn't matter if I'm honest with you since you don't know me and I feel like I can just tell you anything. People are always breaking up. There's nothing special about my situation, and I know that. But in novels and movies, people always get some kind of resolution after they get dumped. I feel adrift. It's 10 p.m. on Wednesday right now, so, call me back. I might try you again in the morning. This is Anna. Thanks.

Jeff closed his eyes and pressed down on his eyelids with his fingertips. We were both still half-naked, which made me laugh even more than the sounds of bachelors throwing hissy fits on television. Jeff smiled and handed me my skirt. 'I'm sorry I yelled at you. I think you should go now.'

'Is there anyone? Anyone you're seeing?'

'I don't owe her an answer. Just leave, please.'

I went home and rushed to the bathroom. On the toilet, I browsed Quora on my phone. I like answering personal questions for strangers. I like feeling helpful and having a sense of purpose. 'Why do I feel the light even after closing my eyes completely?' someone had asked. Don't you mean *see* the light, I wrote in response, and got down-voted within seconds. Someone else explained that darkness wasn't an absence of light but the receptors in our eyes reacting to the closing of eyelids. Everyone appreciated this answer despite its irrelevance.

'Can cats sense sadness?' I once asked, but no one posted a response. I Googled the question and learned that cats can read facial expressions. They avoid sad people. When I cried, Boccaccio would stand on all fours and stare at my face. Perhaps he was trying to figure out what emotion I was expressing. The only time I saw my mother cry was when she thought I was asleep but I'd woken up for a glass of water. The next morning she told me my father had returned to Bangalore. We never heard from him again.

I got ready for bed and put on pajamas which had small elephants printed on them. Boccaccio liked climbing onto the bed and placing himself on my lower belly at sunrise each morning. I would roll onto my side while he scrambled to maintain his footing, digging his claws into the blanket until he found a comfortable position. Sometimes he landed awkwardly with his front paws on my hip and his back paws on the edge of the bed frame. Even so, he remained perfectly still and gently lowered his chin onto his paws. It is impossible for a cat to be clumsy, just as it is impossible for babies to be ugly.

Usually I don't take my phone to bed, but I was feeling restless, so I looked for more newly posted questions on Quora in the Domestic Animals section. Do abandoned cats get upset? If I raised a lion like a domestic cat, would it eventually love me or kill me? Can a dog go senile? Am I just fooling myself when I think that my cat feels affection for me? How long will it take for my ex-boyfriend's dog to forget me? I didn't have answers to any of the questions, so I logged off Quora and downloaded a moodtracker app. I rated my mood as a five out of ten. According to the app, the national average mood was 4.82.

There were questions I would never post on Quora, like what if you never really liked boys but you dated one in high school because that's how you knew to fit in? What if you let the boy take your virginity at sixteen? What if you had an orgasm but the boy himself left you cold? What if years later he was accused of raping a woman you knew in high school? What then? Were you culpable because you couldn't tell the difference between a request and coercion, or because saying no could make you visible and the boy had friends whose laughter sounded through hallways like an authoritative reminder? I've typed the question often, but never posted it. If I had to, perhaps it would be categorised under *law and ethics*.

Anna hadn't called me back, so I sent her a text. *I'm srry I cudn't get the info. Will return yr cash.* I closed my eyes but stayed awake.

PRINCIPLES OF PREDICTION

The phrase *when it rains it pours* frustrates me because there are different varieties of rain. Sometimes it pours, but sometimes it drizzles. Today it falls in pellets. The diagrams flashing across my computer go from orange to red, and finally a bright mass of static insinuates itself at the edges of the screen. For a moment, I'm engulfed like someone discovering a hidden room in a video game. I wonder whether I am losing my sight and call my supervisor over to my desk. His name is Antony, and he has a bald patch on his left cheek where his beard refuses to grow. In real life, there are no panic buttons or giant tickers counting down to apocalyptic storms. I've never seen anything like this and ask Antony what he thinks we should do with our final days. He looks at me as though I'm contagious. 'Go home and get some rest,' he says.

I see Rahul's Hyundai parked outside our house. We live in a bungalow on the outskirts of Bombay. He must also be home early from Mantel & Co., where he is chief design consultant: he makes toys for a living. He thinks contemporary dolls are despondent and believes in the singularity – not the kind where the universe reverts to its primal state but the kind where technology develops a consciousness. Rahul creates possibilities for posterity, while I anticipate their annihilation. There is a police car parked by his Hyundai.

The front door is open and two uniformed policemen are questioning Rahul. He gestures toward me and says something I can't hear. The police hover as Rahul hugs me and asks me to sit down on the sofa. Rahul and I rarely display affection, and the unexpected gesture of tenderness frightens me.

'Your mother is missing,' he says. 'Well, actually, she's absconding. She left a note addressed to you.'

'I already know what it says,' I tell him. I scrunch up the note in my fist to emphasise that I don't need to read my mother's parting words. I don't want Rahul to think he knows more about my mother than I do. It is the only upper hand I have when we argue about her interference in our lives. She always needs to be the centre of attention.

I ask for water and lie down on the sofa. The policemen, embarrassed by this demonstration of feminine weakness, refrain from asking me questions. Once Rahul gives them money, they take our leave, promising to return when they have better news. We sit in silence for a few minutes, and Rahul tries to hold my hand but I pull away. He looks hurt. 'I need some time alone,' I say.

I lock myself in the bathroom to read the scrunched-up note. I learn that my mother has vanished with her neighbour's daughter's gold jewellery. She plans to make an offering to lord Shiva for my future children and wants me to take care of her dog whose name is Anarkali. I fold the note and hide it in a stack of banana-fibre sanitary pads.

Rahul and I have been engaged for two years, but we have not set a date for the wedding. My mother did not want me to marry him because our kundali is mismatched – a superstitious practice which I'm not inclined to believe – but still I wear an opal-studded ring on my pinky finger for protection. I believe in science, but I am my mother's daughter after all. When I saw her a few months ago, she said she was consulting with Swamiji about my salvation.

'You don't want to come back as an insect after you die,' she had said.

Not wanting to look at her, I walked over to the glass cabinet where she displayed souvenirs. Porcelain bowls from China, clay animals from Thailand, a plastic dinosaur from America. Places she had been with my father before he left us. I stole a crystal oyster from the cabinet when my mother was not looking. I knew she would notice eventually. Everything is better with the awareness of my mother's disapproval.

'I'm thinking of getting a pet,' my mother said.

'Sasha and I were not allowed to get a dog because you said it was unnecessary and that there were other ways to practise loss.'

'Why do you turn everything into a battle?'

'Do you know why I was mad at you that entire week when I had the flu, even though you allowed me to stay home and tried to take care of me? I was never actually mad at you. I didn't talk to you and I didn't want you to come near me that week because I didn't want you to get the flu.'

'I spent my life's savings on your education, and this is how you speak to me?'

'I did not come first in my class because you spent thousands of rupees on gifts for that conman. I worked hard and earned my scholarship on merit. Why do you always diminish my achievements?'

'Don't say such things about Swamiji. I don't want to think about where we would be without his guidance.'

That was the last time I saw my mother. We spent the rest of the evening in silence, watching a split-timeline movie about a middle-aged couple whose marriage falls apart.

Rahul drives to my mother's house in Pune and brings Anarkali back. She is a wiry-haired dachshund. I buy plastic covering for all the sofas and take time off from work. My supervisor sends me a flurry of emails, which I don't open even though the subject lines say things like *requiring your urgent attention* and *climate crisis news*. Antony and I never talked about climate change because our work is limited to collecting data and anticipating hyperlocal weather events. We don't speculate on a large scale.

I spend the afternoons not working, cooking elaborate dinners. The weather continues without me. It is July. Anarkali spends her days prostrate by the front door with her torso pressed to the floor as though weighed down by something. When the doorbell rings, she wags her tail, sweeping the floor with it. In the mornings I find her sleeping outside our bedroom door, ensuring we don't abandon her in the middle of the night.

'She seems depressed,' I tell Rahul.

'She needs her mother.'

I am unsure whether he means my mother, who raised Anarkali, or the old dog at the farm in Pune from where she was adopted.

'I'm scared,' I tell him, as we lie next to each other in bed.

'Swamiji can be handled,' he says.

'I don't want Swamiji taken care of,' I say.

'What happened?'

'I guess she really thought it was the right thing to do.'

'I mean, what happened to you and me? This is supposed to be the honeymoon phase.'

'Are we ever getting married? You refuse to pick a date.'

'Your mother's Swamiji was the one who kept saying the timing wasn't right.'

'Now you want to blame her?'

'I'm sorry.'

'Do you like the cold?'

'Is this a philosophical question?'

'I mean, what's your favourite kind of weather? I like the predictable kind.'

Rahul laughs but doesn't say anything. He places his hand on my arm and I hold still. He is always the one to initiate sex. I am thirty-two, and we have been together for five years; it should not be this difficult. A lizard flits across the ceiling like a slow comet. I remember glow-in-the-dark stars on the ceiling of my childhood bedroom. Over the years, everything about that room has transformed: new wallpaper, bedsheets, furniture suited to an adult, everything except stars glued to the sloped ceiling.

My job requires collecting and analysing data over months and months, then compiling the results and predicting storms based on computer-generated models. Of course, my knowledge of the future doesn't come with power, money or the ability to prevent catastrophes. Instead, there's a helplessness, like getting stung by a bee whose erratic movements you've been watching. The ability to predict the likelihood of a cyclone, a break-up, a collapse, doesn't change your lack of control over the event. It is possible to know where and when the storm will arrive, but difficult to assess its intensity.

There is a guava tree on the sidewalk next to our house, and the branches teeter onto our property. Children throw stones at the tree and they clatter against our windows like hailstones. Nothing has broken yet. But it's a nuisance. Perhaps a security guard could be stationed in the area. I imagine the tree being uprooted by a strong gust of wind. The branches would come crashing through our windows, scattering glass everywhere.

While Rahul is scouring Chor Bazaar for Chinese oddities and my sister is teaching marketing to nineteen-year-olds, I make the opposite of a bucket list. A list of things I will never do, in order to give my life direction. I will not procreate. I will not exercise restraint with food because there's no perfect body type when faced with large-scale weather systems, not even a swimmer's body. I will not worry about dolls and objects devoid of sentimental value. I will not look for my mother.

'Rahul does not appreciate me and we have sex once a week like clockwork,' I tell my sister over the phone. He does not bring me gifts, and I've stopped wearing my engagement ring as well as the opal ring. The guava tree taunts me. There is a story about a man who climbed a guava tree and refused to come down because he was afraid of wolves. He was so focused on the wolves that he didn't notice the hornets' nest.

Sasha asks, 'What makes you stay with him?'

'He knows how to comfort me, and isn't that what matters most?'

Sasha is not convinced.

'Are you near a window,' I ask her.

'I'm in the staffroom at work.'

'Stay away from windows. Try to move your desk closer to the exit.'

'I called Ma's phone last night and it rang twice but then it stopped, and now it's unavailable.'

'The police are looking for her. I'm not worried,' I say. I feel protective of my sister because we are both temporary orphans.

'Is Rahul still working nights on the weekends too?'

'I'm about to get into a lift,' I say, hanging up the phone, even though Sasha knows I'm in my kitchen.

Rahul and I continue to live together through the unrelenting monsoon. The sex is hotter now that we are not bound to each other. My mother is still missing. The policemen return from time to time and Rahul pays them to stop harassing us. These days our interactions are friendly. I serve them tea. Rahul leaves the money in a white envelope on the dining-room table. One of them takes pity and gives me the phone number of a detective in Pune. 'He's smart like a hound,' the policeman says. 'He can sniff around and tell you the odds of getting your mother back alive.'

'Why would she not be alive,' I say, my voice a pitch higher than usual.

'No need to panic,' he says, looking out the window. The branches of the guava tree sway in a light breeze, and sunlight is scarce.

One night Rahul asks, 'What do you do when you're sad?' The question is strange in its simplicity, belonging to that category of things you can ask only in the beginning stages of a relationship: What is your last name? What is your favourite colour? Are your grandparents still alive? I do not have an accurate answer to Rahul's question because my emotions often engulf me like a natural disaster, the symptoms clear only in the aftermath. 'Kulfi,' I say, 'with mango.' Some things cannot be asked between people who are familiar to each other.

It rains and we go out for ice cream. Rahul says, 'I watched a documentary about the largest crocodile. His name was Gustave, and he was so big that he was damaging the ecology and needed to be killed. In the documentary, they bait Gustave with a goat, and he goes over to the goat's cage during a rainstorm, but there's a problem with the camera, and the next day Gustave and the goat have vanished. The film ends there.'

'That sounds like a modernist folktale.'

'No,' Rahul says, 'it really happened. I watched the documentary.'

'A woman wanted to perform absence and so she built a boat of ice and rowed until it melted,' I tell him. 'It really happened.'

I call the detective and we agree to meet at my mother's house. I take Anarkali with me in the car. She curls up in the backseat for the entirety of the two-hour drive. When I show up, the detective is waiting outside the gate. He asks me to stay in my car with the dog, and speaks to me through the open window while standing two feet away. 'Looks like rain,' he says in Marathi. 'You'd be well-advised to stay put with the dog. Don't want to get drenched,' he adds. He modulates his voice to make his words sound like a threat, but I realise he's afraid of Anarkali.

I hand him the keys and listen to news podcasts while waiting. No one seems to be speaking about the arriving catastrophe that will leave half the city underwater. Anarkali presses her nose against the car window and gazes at the house as though it might disappear if she looks away. The detective emerges after three hours, smelling of cigarette smoke, and says he cannot help me. There are food stains on the front of his white shirt.

I take Anarkali into the house after he leaves. She runs into my mother's bedroom and darts around frantically. I cannot tell whether she's chasing or being chased by an imaginary entity. Above the bed, there is a large replica of a painting by Dilip Huston called 'Defamation'. The painting haunted me for much of my childhood because of its incoherence: vivid reds and pinks knifed across the canvas. I could not defeat a monster whose form I did not recognise. In my mother's absence, the painting seems ominous, like a heat map dominated by one glaring shade of hazard red.

In my mother's armoire I find a box of keepsakes: souvenirs from places she went without my father, an old diary, a harmonica. I take them with me for safekeeping. I have one waterproof metal trunk where I store things with sentimental value, in case of a flood.

On the coffee table in the living room, my mother kept an unused ashtray. For guests, she insisted, even though she never had any. The detective has left behind a pile of ash, cigarette butts and potato-chip wrappers. I clean up behind him, feeling responsible for the mess.

An old boyfriend once told me that my desire to master the art of storm prediction came from an inability to predict my mother's angry moods. He meant to hurt me, to belittle my obsession with work, but I take relief in blaming my mother for everything. The day I am having, my migraines, the storm that will arrive and destroy everything.

Outside, it is raining. It has not stopped raining for weeks. It does not intend to stop raining. I collect rejected storm names and suggest them to my friends as baby names: Pipal, Bier, Santosh, Siri, Kathak, Rocky, Govinda, Gulbadan. The naming of storms is a democratic process. It is also a delicate matter because storms cause destruction and their names cannot be repeated. I will suggest naming the storm Rahul, even though I know this will be rejected. Storms are always named after women, but people feel more threatened by weather events with masculine names.

On Saturday afternoon, Antony visits me at home. I pretend to be ill and cover myself with blankets as he sits next to me on the sofa.

'It's a good day to launch a satellite,' I joke, thinking of Mr Markawalia.

Antony and I would often make fun of Mr Markawalia's excessive punctuality and his tiny nose. He worked with the Indian National Space Centre. We share resources with them because they maintain the satellites that collect data for our forecast models. Mr Markawalia decides what time a rocket or satellite should be launched based on what his astrologer says would be the most auspicious hour. On occasion, this disrupts everyone's lunch schedule, and all the employees dislike Mr Markawalia. My mother and Mr Markawalia would get along. I have considered introducing them, but now it is too late.

My thighs sweat and stick to the plastic. Anarkali the dachshund jumps up and buries her nose in Antony's armpit, but he pretends it is the most natural thing in the world. He once told me his childhood dream was to be a landscape architect, and he still reads extensively about plants and gardening. He lives alone in a small studio. He does not have a garden, and his potted sunflower recently died.

'Relationships are like plants,' I tell Antony.

'Yes,' he says, 'but sunflowers can re-seed once they've disintegrated.'

At first I think he means to say recede, and I laugh, but later realise what he meant. It is October, and the rain should be receding.

Antony's favourite word is tempestuous. I've never heard anyone use that word with such frequency in everyday conversation. His health, the political climate, his first marriage, the soap opera he watches every weekday evening, are all tempestuous. 'You've had a tempestuous couple of months,' he says.

'Do you think it is easier when someone dies than when they disappear?' I ask Antony before trying to kiss him. My lips land on the bald spot on his left cheek. He says nothing, and leaves after giving me a letter notifying me that I am no longer employed by the National Prediction Centre.

I run outside. He is getting into his car and I yell his name. 'Is the storm still on schedule?' I ask.

Antony shakes his head. 'That was an anomaly,' he says. 'A prediction error in the calculations.' A strong gust of wind causes him to take a few steps back, and I know he is lying because he rubs his left cheek.

I call Rahul, and when he answers, his voice sounds distant.

When I ask about the woman's voice in the background, he says he is at the dentist's. 'Do you have a toothache?' I ask.

'It's nothing,' he says.

'I lost my job,' I tell him, and he seems unsurprised.

There is a manufacturing error at Mantel & Co. Rahul brings home a box filled with a dozen snowless snowglobes. When you shake them the right way, a hurricane forms in the centre. I keep one on the table on my side of the bed. The rest I give away to the postman, the milkman, the boy who delivers eggs and bread. They seem surprised, and the boy asks in slow English, 'What is the reason of this?'

'It's something pretty,' I tell him, and for a moment I see my madness in the expression on his face.

The house is littered with dysfunctional toys that Rahul brings home from work. Miniature houses without any doors, unicorn headbands that are too phallic, dolls accidentally embedded with magnets. I realise that I am like these toys – a project that did not work out. I start seeing a therapist because I know I am more malleable than plastic or metal. My therapist is a small, bubbly woman and she annoys me.

I quit therapy after a month. I stop taking showers. I buy an egg timer to help me meditate in the mornings. The timer makes a soft ticking sound that starts following me everywhere, even when I'm not at home. One morning, the buzzing of the egg timer induces a panic attack. Rahul finds me on the kitchen floor with my head inside the refrigerator. 'I'm trying to cool down,' I tell him. I beg him to learn how to swim instead of wasting his days building toys.

'You're smarter than this,' he says.

I have a headache and can barely breathe. 'Physiological signs of a shift in air pressure,' I tell Rahul. He runs his fingers through my hair, but keeps his torso at a distance, as though I'm a large, unwieldy animal with claws.

I do not expect to survive the storm, which I have christened Garuda, the mythological king of birds.

The week before the storm, I compulsively turn off the electrical mains before we go to bed. I don't want to be electrocuted in my sleep. The ice in the fridge melts, and water seeps into the packets of semi-frozen vegetables and fruit pulp. The milk goes bad. 'We'll die of food poisoning before anything else,' Rahul says. He stubs his toe in the dark one night, and we no longer talk before falling asleep. I hold on to his arm with one hand and the edge of the mattress with the other.

On the predicted day, I stand outside under the whipped cream clouds and wait for the city to overturn. My mother has been missing for one hundred and seventy days, which makes her reappearance unlikely. She liked to sleep with the windows open, so her dreams could take on the lightness of clouds. 'In my next life, I want to return as rain,' she said. I told her she was disorganised enough to return as a hurricane. The storm has no real body, but it is centred, unlike my scattered self, and for this reason I am envious. I keep waiting until my legs go weak and the night arrives. Rahul returns from work and finds me still standing outside and pulls me back into the house. 'They found your mother,' he says, and I feel a twinge of sadness because I will miss Anarkali.

NUMEROLOGY

When I was eight, my parents took me to an astrologer who translated my name into numbers and wrote down seven things on a sheet of paper, which my mother sealed in a light blue envelope, to be opened and read on my thirteenth birthday. I turned thirteen last year, but my mother died a week before the day I was to read the contents of that envelope. It remains unopened, where my mother placed it, between pages sixteen and seventeen of *Alice's Adventures in Wonderland*. Sometimes I open the book and hold the envelope up to the light, but it is unusually opaque. I'll open it on my next birthday because it would be inauspicious to do so any sooner. I read and re-read pages sixteen and seventeen, searching for some hint of my mother, a secret code, but all I find is a scene about Alice shrinking and imagining herself as a telescope.

For a while I resented Rani for dying so near my birthday, as though it had been a choice. She could have waited, I thought. She could have let me have my party and then scolded me for having my friends over past midnight, and then felt guilty and taken me out for sitaphal milkshakes from Apsara Ice-cream Parlour. Instead, I spent my birthday with Mina Aunty (my father's sister) while my father and brother were at the crematorium.

My brother Rajiv is already eighteen, and sometimes I am jealous because he had Rani for five years more than I did. 'An average body uses three hundred kilograms of wood to burn,' he told me when they returned from the cremation. 'Family is like a ship,' he added, 'we have to work together or we sink.'

Tomorrow I turn fourteen, and my best friends – Laila and Neetu – will come over for dinner. Tomorrow I will open the envelope.

Rani had unruly hair, which would frizz during the monsoon months. Einstein hair. My hair stays straight and thin regardless of the weather. Sometimes my father called her raat ki rani – queen of the night – when she was in a dark mood. There was always something a bit sombre about her. It emanated from her eyes, and I did not see it in the faces of the mothers of my friends. That was how I knew Rani was different.

Father and I play a game where he tells me untruths and I pretend to believe him, except sometimes I think I do believe the things he claims. We loved playing this game when I was younger and still developing a grasp over language. Back then I didn't expect words to hold the possibility for deception. Bombay used to be seven islands until the islands were pushed together by the strongest man in the world. Spanish is the language of rivers, and birds communicate through wind patterns. The colour and intensity of sunlight depends on the collective mood of a city's inhabitants. Rain water contains spirits of the dead. Chickens have four legs and two are invisible in order to make them appear bird-like. Some squirrels are mystics.

There is a scar on my father's wrist that he sometimes claims to have received from fighting off a mugger, while other times it's from a hot stove, a malfunctioning firecracker, or saving a kidnapped baby. He once said the scar was from falling in love.

'How is that possible,' I said.

'Love is vicious.'

'You got it in a fight with Rani?'

'No, the mark simply appeared when I fell in love with her, on our second date. Something about the way she ate cheese toast made me want a lifetime of meals with her.'

'You're lying. Rani never liked cheese toast.'

I regretted my words, even as I heard them emerge from my mouth. My father looked stunned, as if the lie had merged with an actual memory and I was challenging everything he remembered.

'Tastes change,' he said after a brief pause, and I didn't push the matter any further.

Rani was reduced to ashes. I like to imagine that she is the dust on the windowpane in my room, obscuring my view of the building being constructed across the street from our house.

I am impatient. I have decided to open the blue envelope tonight instead of waiting until tomorrow. Rani didn't believe in numerology or occult practices for most of her life, but something came over her in the months before her death. 'A displaced anxiety,' I'd heard my father whisper over the phone to my grandmother. Father and I reach a compromise. 'Open the envelope at midnight,' he says, even though it is already my birthday in fifteen countries.

Elvis Presley and Stephen Hawking share a birthday with me. Perhaps this means I am destined to be like them, but most likely I will grow up to resemble my parents. The thought was once terrifying, because it was fashionable among my friends to complain about our parents. Now I know it would be a way of keeping Rani with me, even though my father says he doesn't want me to have her genes. 'I want you to be happy,' he says.

Elvis Presley's mother made shirts in a garment factory and cleaned hospital floors while dreaming of becoming a model. Laila says every generation is better looking than their parents, but only in the case of love marriages. Laila's mother is the most beautiful woman I know.

I spend the evening on the living-room sofa, flipping through the pages of a book that was given to me on my thirteenth birthday. My father tries to engage me in conversation. 'What did you do in school,' he asks.

'We had a special biology lesson,' I say, and he doesn't ask any more questions.

The guest lecturer was Laila's mother, who volunteers as a counsellor at our school. She told us things we already knew, about sex and the differences between male and female body parts. At the end of the lesson, we were encouraged to write down questions on a piece of paper and pass them to the front of the classroom, where Laila's mother would read and answer them. 'Is it true that menstrual blood is a phantom being?' I wrote. I had read this in a textbook from Rani's bookshelf. She taught anthropology at a local college and let me browse through her books, even the ones about mating rituals, perhaps to counteract the effects of my father's lying game.

Some of the pieces of paper with our anonymous questions were quietly disposed of, including mine, but we learned that oral sex does not cause pregnancy, regardless of whether you spit or swallow. I later retrieved the unanswered questions from the wastepaper basket. Most of them were about sex toys or jokes about sex with animals. One said, 'What if sex is the only proof of love?'

My father falls asleep in his chair at 11.30 p.m. and I stare at the muted television screen where a young girl seems weighed down by the sparkly, embroidered dress she has been made to wear.

At midnight, I wake my father. 'Birthday,' he exclaims. 'Happy Birthday.' I am still clutching the book with the envelope, as if it might attempt an escape. I open the envelope and unfold the sheet of unlined notebook paper. The writing seems to be in a script I cannot understand, and this causes me to panic. I look closer and recognise a few words: strength, optimism, path. The writing is in English, but mostly illegible.

I show my father the paper and he squints at it with great concentration. 'What does it say?' I ask.

'I don't know. It looks like Sanskrit. I think it says you-look-like-a-monkey. Right there.'

'Stop it. Just stop. It's not a game.'

'Wait, I didn't mean to…'

I slam the door to my room. I can hear his footsteps in the hallway. He hesitates outside my door, and then walks over to my mother's bedroom, which is now just his bedroom. In my mind, it still belongs to her because while she was alive she spent the most time there. He would be at work, and she would read or knit while singing along to Lata Mangeshkar songs from the sixties and seventies.

Rajiv is away at college. He sends me an e-card with a talking unicorn. I receive five birthday cards, two bars of Cadbury milk chocolate and one Chinese ink pen from my classmates. Laila and Neetu come over after school and we order a pizza. I bring out a large box filled with party supplies from last year. Forty unused party hats, confetti cans, whistles, a pink pony piñata, gift bags for the guests with custom-made diaries that say *Samba's Thirteenth Birthday* on the cover. We each wear five party hats and binge on tamarind sweets, candy cigarettes and bullseye peppermints. The confetti is disappointing.

'I have something for you,' my father says, when I bring him a slice of pizza.

'Not now,' I tell him, hoping he hasn't forgotten his promise to let me have my friends over as late as I want.

He looks bewildered and I feel guilty. 'What is it,' I say, my voice harsher than I had intended.

'The paper from the numerologist. I went back there. She's really old, but she helped me decipher her handwriting. I have it printed out, and I thought you might want to see it, but I can see you're busy.'

'No, I want it now.'

You are seeking truth.
Do not stray from your path.
Study science or law.
Do not be too sensitive to life's obstacles.
True love is difficult for you.
Always beware of the evil eye or grapes danger.
Unknown.

'Grapes,' I say, after reading the list.

'I told you she's old,' my father says. 'Her eyesight is weak.'

'What about the seventh line?'

'She had no idea what it said.'

'Thanks. I should get back to my friends.'

'Okay, have fun. The cake is in the fridge. Mina Aunty sent it, and she called earlier. You should call her back.'

'I'll call her after dinner.'

'You look beautiful. So grown up. Your mother would have been proud of you.'

'Do you think Rani's death was my fault?'

'What are you talking about? It was an accident.'

'I know what happened.' I force myself to say the words, and my voice sounds cartoonish. 'She killed herself.'

'Shut up, Samba. You don't know anything.'

I go back to the dining table, where Laila and Neetu are gossiping about Jai. He is the tallest boy in our class, and everyone thinks he is mysterious because he has seen a dead body.

Neetu blows into a whistle; the kind with a colourful tail that unfurls. 'Time for cake,' she says.

I announce that Jai will be my first kiss. It becomes the seventh fortune on my list.

ELEPHANT MAXIMUS

Chor Bazaar, located near Bombay's Mutton Street, translates literally as thief market. This is a misnomer since it is not the thieves but their wares that are for sale. The market is a well-organised place. Sector A (across from the parking lot): Bags and jewellery. Sector B (keep walking): Cars and electronics. Sector C (turn left twice): Furniture. Squatting in unclaimed territory between Sector A and Sector B, Cassata's father, as everyone knows, sells stolen shoes. His neighbours call him a fraud because shoes are the easiest item to steal in a city with so many temples.

Cassata used to accompany her father on his temple visits. First, they would remove their ten-rupee Bata flip-flops at the temple gates. Then, after a few directionless steps, never going beyond the entrance, 'Find your chappals and let's go,' Cassata's father would say loudly. This was her cue to search the sea of boots, sneakers, sandals and designer heels for the best-looking pair. Once that was accomplished, Cassata and her father would walk home in the ill-fitting shoes of strangers; Bata flip-flops left behind, and feet blistering.

Shoes are a dangerous speciality despite the ease with which they can be procured. Cassata learned this when she was twelve years old. A classmate had pointed at her shiny black rubber boots and said, in a tone that was more curious than accusatory: 'Those are mine.' There were no real consequences apart from the embarrassment Cassata felt when everyone within earshot turned to stare at her. Unlike bags or cell phones, people recognise their footwear on someone else. Cassata stopped wearing stolen shoes and decided to find a speciality of her own.

For six months she turned into an aimless kleptomaniac. Stealing a variety of objects like blouses, homeopathic medicine, automobile magazines, cutlery, musical instruments, baby strollers, sandwich board signs, oil paintings, boxes of samosas and kaju katli, and a small merry-go-round. She even tried stealing the usefulness of things by taking the tops off salt-and-pepper shakers, seats from bicycles and steering wheels from cars. Most of the things she stole were quickly abandoned, except for the stroller, which she used to wheel around a small stuffed toy rabbit – the only toy she'd ever been bought from a department store by an aunt who never visited again.

One day, a cat jumped into the stroller and curled itself around the rabbit as though they were long-lost twins. Animals are such wise creatures, Cassata thought. She realised stealing inanimate objects would never allow her to reach her full potential. 'Are you your best self?' her teacher often asked when she went to class without her homework. Cassata resolved to become an expert at animal theft.

She borrowed animal encyclopaedias and manuals about petcare from the bookseller across from her father's shoe shop. The bookseller always tore out the pages about animal reproduction and genitalia before giving Cassata the books. She could tell from the index which chapters had been removed. Cassata told her best friend, Sai, that she was a cat burglar. He understood what she meant and corrected her, even though he did not believe her. 'You're a cat-napper,' he said. 'Not a burglar.'

At first, her father had disapproved. 'There are stray cats and dogs and goats everywhere. No one pays money for things they can find on the street,' he argued. But Cassata had an eye for well-trained, good-looking animals. The kind children throw tantrums for, the kind that won't pee on sofas.

Cassata took an animal only when she thought its owner was neglectful. Hungry-looking cats, dogs left waiting in cars, wandering turtles. Sometimes she stole chickens from the butcher and sold them back to him at a bargain price. When she was fifteen, she found a cobra and de-fanged it with the help of a Special Edition *National Geographic*. She learned not to do this again, because without its fangs, the snake died of starvation.

The first animal Cassata ever stole was a white cat with mismatched eyes. She found it cowering under a parked car. A blue string around its neck was the only sign that it belonged to someone else. Cassata simply lifted the cat into her arms and walked off. Excessively soft fur, as she later learned, was also an indicator of a domesticated cat. A store-bought pet shampoo is required to achieve that level of silkiness. A day after a hand-drawn Kitten For Sale sign went up outside the shoe shop, a young man in a Fiat bought the cat for two hundred rupees.

Cassata once found a 'MISSING' poster advertising a large reward for a Pomeranian that was in her possession. She decided to return the dog, but felt too embarrassed to accept the money. The Pomeranian's owner, a small woman, insisted on telling Cassata her life story: 'I used to be a Kathak dancer. I was famous in the South. I didn't have time to get married, and now I live alone, with this furry little person. I trained him to walk himself every evening since my knees are no good now.'

Cassata was barely fourteen when she became a well-known figure in Chor Bazaar. The other sellers regarded her with respect. People came to her with requests for certain breeds, but she refused because it went against her work ethic. She made an exception if the customer was a parent looking to replace a deceased pet in order to avoid dealing with their child's questions about death.

Sai still did not believe Cassata's stories about abducting animals. He told her she had a vivid imagination, which is something his parents had often said to him when he was younger.

Cassata watched innumerable Hollywood romances dubbed in Hindi, and tried to understand the notion of Love. Sai held a majority stake in her heart, but she remained unsure whether it was the same thing women in romance movies experienced. Not wanting to lose Sai to someone else, she constructed a list of scenarios, each ending with Sai asking for her hand in marriage:

#1 Serenade. Preferably with large drum or portable music machine.

#2 ~~Earn~~ ~~Steal~~ Find enough money, the rest will follow.

#3 Follow him around like a puppy.

The third item on Cassata's list was inspired by Vodafone's advertising campaign featuring an ugly miniature pug. The entire city was fixated on watching the Vodafone puppy as he chased behind his young mistress for thirty seconds, between episodes of *Indian Idol*. Cassata decided on a scenario which involved stealing the Vodafone puppy to give to Sai as a gift. Animals often took a liking to her because she was small but unafraid to scratch or bite back when they did. Most creatures, she sensed, were happier in her possession.

Vodafone's customer service line did not officially have any information on the pug's whereabouts, nor did they seem willing to release any if they had it, but the lady on the phone revealed to Cassata that her cousin knew the dog's owners. Cassata got an address from the lady after announcing, in an affectedly sad voice, that her mother had abandoned her.

The Vodafone puppy – his real name was Rocky – was being walked by his personal trainer when Cassata took him. She blended in with a gathering of schoolgirls who had been trailing behind Rocky and his trainer, before running ahead of them. Cassata was at that precise age when intelligence co-mingles with the remnants of baby fat. Her childlike features belied her cunning. She planted herself in front of Rocky and his well-chiselled trainer, and began yelling her head off:

'KUTTA CHOR!'

The trainer stood motionless, reminding Cassata of a Romanesque sculpture. Perhaps he was contemplating the ways in which he could salvage the situation; perhaps he was fearful that passersby would misconstrue the scene, leading to unwanted consequences; or perhaps he was simply wondering why this chubby young girl was calling him both a dog and a thief? There exists an unbridgeable abyss between the language of children and the language adults believe them to be speaking. What Cassata was really screaming was:

'Dog-thief!'

In the confusion created by her yelling, Cassata grabbed Rocky's leash and sprinted away. Rocky obediently wobbled after her while the Roman statue remained standing, clutching a plastic bag filled with dog turds.

For an entire week no one noticed Rocky's disappearance, since he still appeared in television spots. The owners assumed he was with the trainer, and the trainer was too humiliated to report the incident. The day after Sai's birthday, his mother showed up at Cassata's house with the puppy. She pretended Cassata was not in the room, and spoke only to her father.

'If you don't control them at this age, they'll just get out of control, you know. Give them a foot and they think it's a mile,' Sai's mother said.

'Yes, I absolutely agree. I'll speak to Cassata about it.'

'It's just the age they're at. Very difficult age. You really need to keep tabs on them. She can't just go around giving out puppies, you know.'

'I know, I couldn't agree more.'

Sai's mother spoke rapid English like Cassata's teachers at school and the foreigners in television shows. Her father responded with stock phrases he'd memorised, which he sometimes heard from customers. Yes. This is too much. We have a deal. Thank you. Their conversation followed this pattern for ten long minutes until Sai's mother left, taking the dog with her. Cassata's father told her to be more careful. 'Don't get me into trouble,' he said. Cassata knew her father cared about her well-being, but sometimes she wished he cared about the things her friends' parents cared about, like report cards and career counselling.

The next day, Sai apologised for his mother's behaviour. 'I love the puppy. He is always happy,' Sai said, incredulous.

'You're welcome,' Cassata said. 'Do you believe me now?'

'Do I believe you about what?'

'That I'm a cat burglar.' She smiled.

Sai paused to consider the implications of this. 'You *kidnapped* Rocky from someone?'

Cassata looked into his eyes with intensity – the way she had seen it done in movies, when someone is about to confess their love. She wasn't sure whether she actually felt love, but she'd always wanted to enact it. 'Sai, I would do anything for you,' she said. 'I would steal an elephant. A koala bear. An entire zoo.'

'You would steal an elephant for me?'

'Yes.'

'Liar. Prove it.'

'What?'

'I said, prove it. Steal an elephant for me.'

Cassata wasn't sure how to respond. She was a pet-napper but she was not a liar. 'Okay,' she said.

She spent weeks reading about elephant habits and habitats. The bookseller would not let her read about elephant sex. She roamed the city to no avail, hoping she might find a trained elephant that tourists paid to joyride.

Two months after Sai asked Cassata for an elephant, she is being interviewed by an unfamiliar woman from the local newspaper. A group of animal smugglers had sent an anonymous tip to the police, implicating Cassata for their recent crimes. After spending a week skulking around Cassata's father's shop, the detective assigned to the case realised Cassata was the young girl who brought him cups of tea every evening. Embarrassed, he dropped the case, but a local reporter picked up on the rumour.

'You have an unusual name,' the reporter says.

'My grandfather had a sweet tooth. He died a few days before I was born. Cassata was his favourite cake.'

'Was he also in the business of stealing things?'

Cassata shrugs. She doesn't know. She senses that the reporter is more interested in finding a tragic story than finding the truth of hers.

'And your mother? Where was she through all this?' the reporter asks.

'I don't have a mother. I was a surprise.'

'What do you mean?'

'I mean I was an unexpected delivery.'

There is silence, as the reporter shuffles the papers in front of her.

'I felt really guilty the whole time, because the Indian elephant is an endangered species,' Cassata tells the reporter.

The reporter looks at the notes she had prepared for this interview. 'Yes, well, this elephant you apparently kidnapped—'

'I just took it. Kidnapping suggests that I asked for a ransom, which I didn't.'

'Sorry, this elephant you *took* – no one has actually seen it?'

'I've seen it. I was the one who took it.'

'Apart from you, no one?'

'I guess not.'

'So from what I understand – the zoo is missing an elephant, and you claim to be the one who *took* it, but there's absolutely no proof.'

'I never take animals from the zoo. It's beneath me. But I had to – I did it for love.'

The reporter coughs. 'I'm sorry?'

Cassata wonders why the newspaper sent such an incompetent reporter. 'I stole the elephant for my best friend, Sai. So that he would fall in love with me.'

'Wait, so your best friend – he saw this elephant?'

'He saw the elephant. But he couldn't recognise it. He thought I was the elephant.'

'He thought you were an elephant?'

'No. Well, kind of. I read about something similar once – but he looked right at me, pointed towards the elephant and said, "That's just you disguised as an elephant." And then I couldn't get him to change his mind.'

'So, after that debacle, you sold the elephant to the circus?'

'I had to. My room was buried in elephant shit. But the circus is choosing to deny this, because they don't want to return the elephant to the zoo.'

'I see.'

'Yeah.'

The reporter stares at her notes. She does this each time she asks a question about Cassata's family.

'And your father—?'

'He didn't even notice.'

'Okay. And just so we're clear – you *are* referring to a literal elephant? Large grey creature with tusks?'

'I know what an elephant looks like. I recently stole one from the zoo.'

'Yes, okay. I see.'

Cassata bangs her fist on the table, puncturing the silence. They are in a coffee shop, and the jolt causes her

Coke to fizz. 'That elephant didn't want to be in the zoo; he is a circus elephant. He needs attention.'

'He told you that?'

'Don't be ridiculous. I could sense it.'

'You're an elephant-mindreader now?'

'Not just elephants. All animals.'

The reporter taps her watch without checking the time and says she has to leave. She hugs Cassata and says, 'Bye, doll.'

Cassata thinks the reporter was pleasant but dull, like a flightless bird. She tells her father about the interview. 'That's nice,' he says. Cassata's father has the ingenious ability to process information and react to it without believing or disbelieving. It reminds Cassata of a dog, the way he listens with sweet, sad eyes. Cassata thinks Sai is like a dog too – a cute, yappy one. She wonders why the women on TV sound angry when they say, 'All men are dogs.'

At school, Cassata falls behind on her homework and is made to stand at the back of the classroom, facing the wall. She remains there until lunchtime, and doesn't move even when she feels herself losing control of her bladder and a puddle forms around her feet. The lunch monitor tears out pages from Cassata's empty notebook and places them on the floor around her. After this incident, the English teacher treats Cassata with leniency and refers to her as a sensitive child. She thinks Cassata is misunderstood, even though Cassata does not particularly agree with this assessment. One day, she tells Cassata a story about three blind men attempting to describe an elephant. 'We are like the three blind men,' the English teacher says. 'We cannot see things in their entirety.' Cassata nods and raises her eyebrows as if the fable is a revelation, but she does not understand. According to the doctor who visits their school once a year, Cassata has perfect vision.

Sai does not speak to Cassata in class. They are still best friends, and they talk after school, when Sai walks her home. The elephant incident is a joke between them. 'Is that you disguised as a pigeon on that tree?' Sai asks. 'I am the tree,' Cassata responds. Sai does not know what he saw in Cassata's room.

Cassata is often unable to remember whether an event occurred in a dream, in real life, or on television. She can however, with great acuity, recall every other detail. She remembers being at the zoo and wondering why she hadn't thought of looking for an elephant at the zoo in the first place. The elephant enclosure, when she found it, was empty. The zookeeper, instead of answering her questions, had asked her more questions, such as, Why wasn't she at school? and How did she get past the wire-fence and into the animal enclosure? Cassata had realised that the signposts were mixed up. She had noticed the elephant standing sadly on a grassy patch, claiming to be a family of monkeys.

Cassata still collects cats, but she no longer sells them. She has seven of them, and they are all named Meow.

She sympathises with their plight. Most human beings do not fully understand the feline urge to create chaos by scratching table legs and ripping sofas at their seams, she thinks. She remembers reading a true story about two girls raised by a wolf pack, and wishes she could have grown up in a family of animals. Panthers. They are less frightening than wolves.

The reporter published an article in the local *Sunday Times* supplement, which usually features brunch recipes and celebrity interviews:

'A zookeeper at the Byculla Zoo was arrested earlier this week for failing to report the non-existence of the zoo's elephant. In his statement, he said, "There was never an elephant at this zoo, in the two years I have been employed here." Authorities are searching for the previous zookeeper. They suspect his involvement in an elephant ivory trafficking ring. Kaa, the Byculla Zoo's lone elephant, was reported missing last month by a young girl, who later claimed to have stolen the elephant and sold him to a circus. "We think the previous zookeeper killed Kaa – for his tusks, and also for the meat. Elephant meat is extremely rare and expensive," said the zoo's director. On further questioning, the director added, "The zoo does not get many visitors these days, which is why this information was not brought to our attention earlier."'

Cassata shows Sai this article. Watching him read it, she begins crying soundlessly. Later, Sai will tell her he felt strangely hungry at that moment. 'The only other time I've seen someone cry is when my mother chopped onions,' he will say.

Sai wants to comfort Cassata, but he doesn't know how. She can see him trying. He opens his mouth, but instead of words, an odd sound emerges from his throat. Cassata cannot tell if he is attempting to speak or imitating a whale. She looks at him and says, 'You must believe me.' Sai looks at Cassata's large ears and wonders whether they would function as parachutes if she ever fell from a great height. He has the urge to push her off a precipice, but they are on a sidewalk, so instead he holds her hand.

RADIO STORY

Bombay, 1939

My wife is happiest on Sunday afternoons, when I leave the house. We have been married five years – too soon for us to take pleasure in each other's absence. The boys I spend time with at the Irani Café do not share this sentiment. They believe love and marriage are separate institutions.

Rustom, my best friend, is unmarried; his opinion does not count in these matters. Edalji is older than the rest of us, but his views are biased, since he is trying to find a suitable husband for his nineteen-year-old. Gieve, the fourth member of our amateur radio club, will go to great lengths to get away from his wife. He is not a licenced radio operator, like the rest of us, but he always brings a flask of Black Label to our weekly meetings. The boys call me LK, because my radio call sign is VU2LK. After lunch, we go home and converse only in Morse code, on a frequency no one else has access to. We have voice-capable radio transmitters, of course, but this feels more intimate; our own private language.

These Sundays have no purpose other than food and conversation. We talk about the war, the weather, poetry, women, and occasionally one of the boys will ask me to build or fix a piece of equipment. I run a small radio and acoustics shop where I sell radios, gramophones and guitars. The shop does good business. In fact, some months back, I was able to hire a young man who sits in the shop so I have more free time. 'Why do you need more free time to do nothing?' my wife asks when I spend my days at home, fixing equipment that doesn't require fixing.

This particular Sunday was different. The city was on edge. People were afraid to have conversations in cafés, on trains or buses. The authorities had recently sent notices to every radio operator, revoking our licences and asking us to relinquish all our equipment.

'What's the plan,' Rustom asked, looking at Edalji.

'The plan is to do as we are told, and call ourselves amateur poets or amateur something else.'

'Professional drinkers club,' Gieve said.

My daughter was four, and my wife had become pregnant again two months before. I agreed with Edalji. Rustom taught literary theory at the university, and living without a wife or children left him with too much space in his head. He suggested hiding the equipment. 'We could disassemble our rigs and hide the individual parts.' He had given this some thought.

'To what purpose,' Edalji said.

'I don't know,' Rustom said, and proceeded to tell us about Maya, a colleague of his at the university – a pro-independence protester who had shown interest in establishing an underground radio station to transmit uncensored news. We had emptied the contents of Gieve's flask by this point, and Rustom added that Maya was a 'very fine item'.

Edalji sighed, the way elderly people do when they have grown tired of explaining things over and over to those younger than them. 'Baba, I will find you a nice Parsi girl. Don't worry. Find something else meantime.'

Rustom came to my flat later that evening. When I saw him through the peephole, standing outside my door, I considered pretending I wasn't home and asking my wife to make an excuse for me. But my wife, the chartered accountant, is unwilling to lie for me. She does not compromise when it comes to these things. She measures her deeds – varying degrees of good and bad – by adding and subtracting numbers in a notebook labelled Karma. 'Why should I be the proxy for your sins?' she would say.

I opened the door to Rustom, sure that I was going to be found out, arrested and sentenced to solitary confinement for what he was about to convince me to do.

'Mr Graham Bell has this invention called the telephone,' I said.

'I don't read the papers,' Rustom said.

'That's why you're still smiling.'

My wife is fond of Rustom. She emerged from the kitchen to ask if he wanted chai-pani. 'Two cups chai please, bhabhi. My friend will also be joining us,' he said.

'I gave Maya your address, she should be here soon,' he said to me. All I said was, 'We can talk in my workshop.'

Ours is a small two-bedroom flat on the second floor of a five-storey building. We have electricity, running water and a private bathroom. My wife shares a room with our daughter, and I have my equipment in the second bedroom, which is also where I sleep. I like to call it my workshop, because this sounds more impressive than just saying that it is my room.

Rustom did not say much until Maya arrived, and even then, he was subdued. The only other person to have this quieting effect on Rustom was his mother. But Maya was not an outspoken Parsi woman like Mrs Printer. She was a frail Gujarati woman; the kind my wife would affectionately force-feed samosas and kachoris. She wore a salwaar-kameez and was not particularly well endowed.

'This could really be something,' she said.

'This?' I said, having forgotten a majority of words.

'If you really think you can build a 40-metre AM transmitter. It's more than anything I expected.'

'I'll need to contact some people and find out if I can get the necessary parts. We'll need money, and you'll have to shift base each week to avoid being tracked.'

'We have funding. It will be difficult finding locations, but I think we will manage.'

Everything she lacked in physicality, Maya more than made up for when she spoke. It didn't matter what she said; it was the way her hands moved, as if her fingers were orchestrating words. I felt nervous, but I attributed it to the plans Maya spoke of, and nothing else. Before leaving, she shook my hand and said, 'Have faith.' A strange thing to hear from a professor of philosophy.

I called one of my suppliers, without thinking, and asked if he could deliver a transistor for a 40-meter. It was a noticeably large order. He said it would take two weeks, maybe longer. Those two weeks went by with Rustom and me dismantling our rigs and hiding the parts – in the hollow spaces inside our beds, in jewellery boxes, in the large tin cans filled with rice and sugar – but mostly I spent that time imagining what Maya would say when I next saw her.

The authorities arrived at our homes – unannounced, but not unexpected – and we handed over the relics of our rigs from years ago, in order to appease them and not arouse suspicion. They conducted the requisite inspection of our cupboards and rooms, found nothing, and left. Edalji, as we later discovered, had given them all his equipment and wanted no part in this. 'If they catch you, they'll break your fingers and you won't be able to turn the radio's knobs, let alone your own knob,' he said to Rustom and me.

'We're going to call it the All-India Radio operation,' Maya said. Two weeks had passed. She and Rustom were at my flat, waiting for the supplier. I resisted the urge to kiss Maya's fingertips. Only snippets of her sentences registered in my brain. 'Communications have been cut off between party workers ... across the country ... people do not know ... state of affairs.' In the midst of this, the phone rang, and my supplier expressed his remorse. 'Next week, surely,' he said.

When Maya and Rustom were about to leave, I offered to teach Maya the basics of ham radio. There was a pause, and she looked at Rustom before saying, 'Rustom has already been teaching me some things.' She gave me two hundred rupees to cover the cost of building the transmitter. We decided to meet once the supplier had delivered.

My wife knew what was going on – that I was undertaking something completely illegal – and chose to ignore it. 'They will not touch a pregnant woman. You do what you want,' she said. But I noticed that she went to the temple more often, and the numbers in her Karma notebook grew larger. More unbalanced.

The day I was expecting the transistor, two policemen arrived at my door. They spoke politely to my wife. 'Routine check, routine check,' they kept repeating, as they upturned furniture and violently sifted through cupboards. Everything they found was heaped in the centre of the living room, as if they were planning a bonfire. My wife yelled, cried and feigned dizziness. They asked me to accompany them 'for questioning'.

I was stripped down to my underwear, made to lie on a giant block of ice, and told that I was going to be left there until I had 'more information to give', which I didn't. My body took a long time to go numb, and when it did, I imagined I was in one of those dreams where you keep falling but never feel the impact of the fall. When they realised I was telling the truth, and didn't know who else was involved in this underground movement, they moved me to Arthur Road Jail, where I spent nine months. My wife sent letters written in pencil, some of the words worn out or erased:

Dear LK,
   Without you, life is   . The house feels   . Why is this
? Nalini asks about you,   and I.
She believes you have   been taken by the fairy.   The
baby is   . I stand outside the   gate sometimes,
with the other, hoping   from a
window   . Do you   my letters? This waiting is   .
terrified   , but I cannot
.   Love,

Dear LK,
   I   your presence, your voice, your.
Our daughter still thinks

.

What can I
? I heard more
and were arrested. I am sorry for,   I should have been
. Look at me,   talking as if
, but I know   we'll   again   . It cannot
otherwise. I am always.

Dear LK,
We have   . She is. Her remind me
of you.   I pray that, and we will
. I have not lost, I still

.

When I was released, I went home, expecting nothing
to have changed. I discovered that I had a three-month-
old daughter. For a week, I could not bring myself to hold
her.

Maya came to see me. It was the third time we had ever been in each other's presence, but something between us felt familiar. She told me what had happened: after my arrest, Rustom found a more reliable source for transmitter parts and built the 40-metre. They broadcast every Friday, for three months, on a frequency of 43.5 megahertz, until an unknown person reported their whereabouts and everyone was arrested. 'The saddest part,' she said, 'was finding out that Rustom had told them everything there was to know about the workings of our operation, and in exchange he was allowed to leave the country.' Maya would be tried in court the next week. After speaking for two hours, she stopped, and we sat next to each other in silence – Maya recovering from the talking and me from the information.

We heard my daughter's wails coming from the other room. 'What's her name?' Maya asked. 'I don't know yet,' I said. My wife had not named our second daughter because she had been waiting for me to return. I kissed Maya, not knowing what else to do. She did not stop me, and we kissed while my daughter cried in the next room. It was not sexual, and it felt as if we were assessing each other like insects, with our lips acting as feelers. She stopped me when my wife's voice came through the wall, singing a lullaby to our daughter.

'I'm not going to say anything in court. I don't know what my sentence will be. You take care.' Maya said this as if the past five minutes had not happened, and then she left. Perhaps this is how karma propagates – you are betrayed, and you betray someone else, and that someone else does the same, ad infinitum.

That night, my wife came into my room and lay down next to me on the bed. Her hands were cold against my skin. 'You were away for a long time and you have needs,' she said. I told her I was hungry, but she didn't respond. She left the room and stopped speaking to me.

We named our daughter Gita, which means song. My wife communicated with me through Gita, who would gurgle appreciatively, because she did not yet comprehend words, only the tone of voice: 'Gita baby, will you ask your father what he wants for dinner?' 'Gita, my raja, someone's on the phone for your father.' 'Gita, my doll, do you think your father knows that we have barely any money left?' When Gita started going to school, my wife would have to speak to me by addressing inanimate objects, or by talking at her own reflection in mirrors and shiny objects.

My shop had been searched and shut down when I was arrested. After independence, I procured a loan and reopened within a few weeks. I re-hired the young man who used to sit in the shop; he was no longer young, only younger than me. On most days, I sat in the shop with him, and he told me about his deaf brother who painted portraits of creatures that were half-man, half-bird and half-tiger. I wondered how one creature could have three halves. Tragic incidents excited him, and I let him recount to me things I had already read about in the papers. It gave him a peculiar pleasure. I did not reapply for my ham radio licence, even though by this time it was possible to do so. The young man tried to ask me questions about my year in solitary, but in this I did not indulge him.

He had been telling me about his neighbour's three-legged dog, when an old man entered the shop. It took me some moments to recognise this man as Gieve. He didn't look at me, and enquired with the young man about the price of a guitar.

'Depends on the make,' the young man said, preparing to begin his usual sales pitch about how a guitar was like a mistress.

'Never mind. I was just wondering,' Gieve said, cutting him off.

'Gieve?' I said, but he didn't acknowledge me, until I repeated his name louder, and the young man, thinking Gieve must be partially deaf, yelled 'Uncleji', and motioned toward me with his head. Gieve finally turned his face to me. He placed his hand over my hand, which was resting on the wooden countertop, as if to confirm that I was made of solid matter. 'Has old age affected your hearing,' I said.

'LK. I wasn't sure. I thought you were dead. I'm taking a new medication. For my joints.' He paused between sentences, as if he wanted to be interrupted. 'Last month. On the radio. They said you were dead. They said VU2LK is a silent key.'

My radio call sign had been assigned to someone else, since I had not reapplied for it. I told Gieve this, and his laugh made me nostalgic.

'What's your name? The one your parents gave you,' he asked.

'My real name is Agam,' I said.

We spoke for a long time, about everything that had occurred in the past years, except Rustom. Gieve told me what he knew about my namesake – the other VU2LK had been close to my age when he died of an unknown illness. I hoped it wasn't a mere bureaucratic error on the part of the deities that controlled death. Perhaps, like Gieve, they had got someone else confused with me. I did not voice these thoughts until much later in the evening, when I was eating dinner with my wife, who still would not speak to me. Her face did not show any sign that suggested she had heard me. Sometimes I think she has developed an ability to block the sound waves specific to my voice from entering her ears.

'VU2LK is a silent key,' I said, the words uncomfortable like sticky toffee in my mouth. 'This means the call sign is available again. I could apply for it.'

When I said this, my wife's fuse finally ran out. She exploded. 'What is wrong with you? It's bad luck to take a dead man's belongings.'

'I'm sorry,' I said.

She asked me if I wanted another roti, and that night we slept in the same bed.

It was 1961. My hair was greying, and my daughters were married with children of their own. Jawaharlal Nehru was still the prime minister. *Mughal-e-Azam* was topping the box office. It was the year of dreams in which my body was encased in a glacier stranded somewhere on the

Atlantic. It was the night we conceived our third daughter, Gul.

Over the years, snow collects on a glacier, weighing down on it, until every last air bubble has been compressed, leaving the glacier airless and blue. The first time I saw Gul, she had just emerged from my wife's body. She struggled for air. She looked blue, like a child-god from Hindu mythology. At first I thought Gul was the glacier from my dreams, in which I was encased. It was only much later that I realised I was the snow in which the glacier was encased.

Mumbai, 1996

At LK's cremation, no one says anything to me. Gita cannot be seen talking to me and Nalini won't, even though – or especially because – he is dead now. People always behave that way at funerals, as though the dead guy is still watching, still judging them. At least Gieve smiles at me. He opens his mouth to say something, but when he sees I've brought my husband with me, he changes his mind.

The last time I saw LK was at Maya's funeral. We hadn't spoken in ten years, and when I read Maya's obituary in the newspaper, I fantasised about a reunion with my father, where I would comfort him, and he would forgive me, and I would stop myself from saying, 'I haven't done anything that requires forgiving.'

My husband is from a Muslim family, and even though my parents adored him when they thought he was just a friend, allowed me to have Ramzaan dinner at his house and invited him to spend Holi with us, when I told them that we were in love and engaged, they stopped acknowledging my existence. They realised that I wasn't asking for permission, I was making a declaration. I was still living with them, and when I finally moved out a month later, my mother broke the silence momentarily to give me a box of my things – photographs, awards for being the fastest sprinter at school, pictures of blue houses I had drawn as a child. I thought it was a gesture of tenderness until she said, 'we won't be needing these any more,' as if the memory of me could be returned, like an ill-fitting dress.

She died so suddenly that we didn't have the chance to say different last words to each other. Mine were: 'Whatever. At least my husband is faithful to me.' In the movie of our lives, this would be the cue for a slap, but she pretended not to hear me. Everyone knew LK was having an affair with Maya. Only Gita, with her selective knowledge of the world, seemed oblivious – a cause, or consequence, of the fact that she was our father's favourite.

Nalini looks at me in a way that reminds me of our mother. I know she thinks I brought Saleem to the funeral for spiteful reasons; I want to tell her that he's here so I don't collapse from crying and embarrass myself the way I did at our mother's funeral. I try to remember the lines from that Gulzar poem LK loved; something about time – how you don't see it coming, going or passing by, but it accumulates in people.

At the house, his dentures sit close-mouthed in a glass of water next to his bed. It is too soon to start packing his things – first there will be thirteen days of mourning. I will live here, in our childhood home, with Nalini and Gita, even though Nalini will not speak to me and Gita will say the bare minimum of words necessary to peacefully co-exist: *Lunch. Dinner. Towels, top shelf. More tea? Flowers. Mouse. Doorbell.* I wonder what happens to a dead person's dentures; I don't think they can be recycled or donated, and I doubt anyone would want to keep them. I remove LK's teeth from the water glass and dry them with a hand-towel. I have an overwhelming urge to make the teeth talk; to make the upper and lower jaws dance like a chattering-teeth novelty toy, but I cannot bring myself to do it. As if in response to this desire, the dentures slip from my hand and land on the floor. When I bend down to retrieve them, I find a typewriter and a shoebox under the bed. I open the box and find it empty. All I find is a page jammed into the typewriter, the words packed together on both sides:

My favourite word is zaum. It was invented by Russian word-scientists because they needed a word that had no meaning. I used to imagine them in a laboratory surrounded by buckets of paper pulp and billions of little vials with words in different colours, and letters in every font lining the walls, and even the gates would be a grid of alphabets. I wanted to be a word scientist. I thought that maybe I could invent the perfect word and it would cure my muteness. Then I found out that the word scientists were just linguists, and most of them worked from home. So I decided to make radios instead.

Radios use frequencies that are below visible light. I imagine them as white rainbows travelling everywhere at the speed of sound. I like to think of my silence as white light, below the frequency of audible sound but holding the entire spectrum of words. Except I can't speak, even when it rains, so I write stories sometimes when there's a thunderstorm. On sunny days I like to read under the mango tree in the backyard or tinker with radio parts in my workshop.

People call me Sig – as in 'Cygnus Olor', the mute swan. There is nothing wrong with the swan's vocal chords, it is even known to let out the occasional snort, but it remains silent for most of its life, and sings one achingly beautiful song right before it dies. I like to think of my stories as swan songs; if I can write something beautiful enough, then maybe I'll be able to find it in me to finally speak out loud.

I'm not the only one with problems though. My best friend, Gieve, has a hole in his heart. He says it's only a physiological hole and it hasn't affected his ability to love. But people are scared of holes, and they're always falling into them while trying to learn more about them, like manholes or black holes. I once asked him if he thought there was an entire galaxy residing in his heart, and he told me to stop taking things so seriously.

Gieve learned sign language so that he could understand me. It was funny at first, when he kept getting the signs mixed up. He apologised to me for a week, and then I realised that he was trying to say he loved me.

It mystifies me when people don't say things out loud, even when they have a voice. My parents never said things out loud. They always said what they didn't mean, in strained voices, but if I had my voice I would say everything out loud. I would buy a dictionary and speak every word.

The girl I love is Maya, and she loves nobody, or so she claims. I wrote to her that I was nobody, and she just laughed. I think she's scared that nobody will ever love her because her nose is too big.

At night when we can't sleep, we talk through our radios. I built her one that can only talk to my radio. She tells me little fibs in the guise of stories and I tap out a response to her in Morse code, even though neither of us knows Morse code. It comforts her, the tap-tap-tap—tap-tap—tap.

I sit on the floor with the empty shoebox, the typewriter and the dentures, reading LK's last words – looking for clues to an unknown puzzle. It is futile, like the mute swan's last song or like trying to find a name for nothingness. Perhaps it is best this way, I think, remembering what LK said to me once: 'Sometimes it is better if you cannot find the right words. In some religions, everything can be destroyed with a word.'

'Everything?'

'Everything.'

'What word is that?'

'No one knows.'

Gita interrupts me. 'Tea?' she says.

'Look what I inherited,' I say, holding up the shoebox and the piece of paper.

Gita takes the page and reads it. 'You know he stopped speaking after she died?'

I want to ask if *she* means Maya or our mother. But I already know.

SMILE, PLEASE

My mother appears in my dreams when I'm about to make an important decision and reaches towards me with blue fingertips. In these recurring dreams, her fingers are twisted at odd angles, but I try not to flinch at her touch. I remind myself that she had hypermobile joints, which means she isn't in pain.

I welcome any glimpse of my mother because she died when I was nine. Last night when she appeared, I averted my gaze and looked at the ground, which was covered in rubble. I recount the dream to Riya, who sits beside me at work. 'My therapist told me most dreams are about sex,' she says.

Riya begins a lot of sentences with 'My therapist told me', as though her association with a doctor of the mind provides more heft to her opinions. Her therapist says many things I disagree with, such as: 'Chyawanprash is delicious' and 'Think about what you want before acting on an impulse'.

I work as a dentist's assistant to Dr Nisha at Happy Smiles. Riya is the office manager. She doubles as our life coach because neither Nisha nor I have been to a therapist.

'Do you want to hear a joke?' I say.

'Do I have a choice?'

'A man goes to his therapist, and the therapist draws a series of shapes and asks him to interpret them. The man keeps saying that each one reminds him of sex. Eventually, the therapist diagnoses him with sex addiction and the man says, "Well, who's the one drawing the dirty pictures."'

'I've heard that one before.'

Bheem enters the clinic, and we stop talking. I lead him to Dr Nisha's consulting room without saying a word because he is the son of Bombay's second-biggest crime lord. In his presence, we are not to mention his father's activities, any current news events, whom we supported in the last election, topics related to ethics and morality, or details of our personal lives (such as where we live). I'm glad for the silence because I feel too nervous to speak around Bheem. It's something between terror and crushing desire.

Dr Nisha specialises in smile improvement therapy. She trains politicians, actors, professors and beauty queens in the art of smiling. Apart from teeth polishing and adult braces, she teaches them how to contort their facial muscles. She calls it yoga for the face, except each session costs an exorbitant amount and I can barely tell the difference in the before and after photographs.

Bheem leaves after a cleaning and some facial exercises, which he'll need to practise daily. Nisha places a palm on her forehead and says, 'I am going to teach this thirty-nine-year-old how to smile or I am going to lose a limb; perhaps they will see him smile and have mercy on me and only take a finger, preferably a toe. Does one get a choice in these matters?'

I shrug and clear the workstation for the next client.

'You seem distracted,' Nisha says. She takes the box of disposable gloves from my hand and places it on the wrong shelf. I will need to rearrange everything after she leaves the office.

'It's nothing,' I say, the dream still fresh in my mind.

I return to my desk and absent-mindedly check my phone every few minutes. Riya rolls her eyes and suggests calling Bheem's number or sending him a photograph on WhatsApp.

'What would I send him a picture of?'

'Send him a poem. I've been reading a book of Urdu poetry,' she says. 'Were you aware that no one actually knows whether the moth is drawn to the flame or trying to attack it? But the former view remains popular because it's more romantic.'

'Salamanders are also attracted to flames.'

'In medieval Persia, people considered salamanders to be birds. It's a matter of perspective.'

'I'm always the last to know things.'

'I hadn't noticed how big your eyes are. They remind me of Brigitte Bardot.'

'I like her gap tooth. I shouldn't say this at work, but gap teeth are cute. I don't understand people who want them fixed.'

'Did you know some people are turned on by dental play?'

'Do you mean biting and stuff like that?'

'No, they're turned on when they get dental work done. I guess it makes sense. If you're into pain, then you'd be into something like getting your teeth pulled.' Riya scrunches her eyebrows and sucks air through her teeth, as though solving a math puzzle.

Later that day, as if prompted by the dream, an email arrives. I'm relieved because the dreams often precede events that are outside of my control, such as hail storms, viral flu, or betrayal by a friend. An email seems innocuous in comparison.

From: sylvia@hotmail.com
To: tanitunes@gmail.com

Dear Tani,

I don't think you would remember me – and you have no reason to, since I was barely a glimmer on the periphery of your lives when you were a newborn, though your mother meant the world to me. She still does, and always has consumed my inner world. After I heard of her untimely death, despite not having been in touch for years (or perhaps for that very reason), I found myself thinking of her more often. As if recollection could reinstate something lost.

Another strange thing about the finality of death: my grief took on a subdued quality after years of anger over this discarded friendship. If I'm honest, I felt discarded when your family drifted away from me. I moved to Kolkata and they stopped calling. Well, perhaps that's an exaggeration. We said our goodbyes when your head was still the size of my palm. If we passed each other in the street, you wouldn't know me and I might mistake you for a ghost. Do you resemble your mother?

Let me get to the point before you stop reading. I'm writing because I'll be in Bombay next week and I have some letters and mementos that belong with you. They are remnants of my friendship with your mother and clues to a different side of her.

I wrote and re-wrote and deleted this email multiple times. In the end, I decided sharing what I could about your mother outweighs the risk of unearthing old wounds. Can anything remain hidden forever? (Your mother would say: What a dramatic line, Sylvia. Put it in a poem.) I hope we can meet, even if only for the briefest.

With love, Syl.

From: tanitunes@gmail.com
To: sylvia@hotmail.com

Dear Sylvia,

I'm grateful for your email and I look forward to the opportunity to talk further about the things you mentioned. There are so many conflicting accounts of the past, it would be cathartic to have something concrete. Something uncontestable.

Due to the circumstances surrounding my mother's death, no trace remains of her. No photographs, no letters. Everything was lost.

I don't remember much about that night, but there's news footage of the incident on YouTube and I can see myself in the background. That's how I know I was there even though for years, throughout my adolescence, I told people I'd survived because I was at a sleepover. Rahul thinks our mother would never have let us go for a sleepover because she worried we'd be molested. I probably wouldn't have been invited to one anyway.

Please get in touch when you're in Bombay.

—T.

For most of my life, I tried to be normal by making decisions like girls who had mothers. As teenagers, these girls seemed to enjoy doing the opposite of what their mothers wanted, and I adopted an identical modus operandi. Belly-button piercing, a tattoo of a dragonfly, a college boyfriend who dropped me home on a motorbike and sneaking alcohol on school trips. These days I pay more attention to what I really desire.

When I dial Bheem's number, I feel the thrill of transgression and the relief of certainty. I have made a decision about what I want. He doesn't sound surprised to hear from me and asks how I'm doing with the warmth of an old friend. He speaks slowly, like someone who commands attention, not the rushed speech of a person with too many siblings.

I invite him over. A moth hovers above my bedside lamp and appears to be in a state of rapture. I wonder whether the moth experiences disappointment when the glass barrier protects him from being burned.

Bheem arrives wearing a white shirt and denim jeans which appear freshly ironed. He steps towards me and I resist the impulse to step back, as though about to tango. Instead, I stand my ground. He holds my chin with the tips of his fingers but doesn't kiss me. I lead him to my bedroom and the rest occurs like a distant dream. My body goes into auto-drive while my brain processes the shocking strangeness of getting naked in front of a man whose last name can only be whispered.

Days pass, but change gives the sensation of months, like walking through darkness and waiting for my eyes to adjust, but they never do. It's a constant feeling of straining to see something in the distance.

Bheem often comes over after midnight because he works late. He tells me he manages the family's legitimate businesses, which include three upscale North Indian restaurants, a construction company and a beauty salon. He attended an International Business Management course in London for three years to train for his role. 'I handle the business,' he says, without specifying what his day-to-day work involves. 'Restaurant business runs late,' he insists. Most days he smells of rum and mutton kebabs, but occasionally of cement dust.

A few weeks into our affair, Bheem comes to Happy Smiles for a check-up. I want to flaunt the new closeness between us and simultaneously keep it hidden like something that fades in sunlight. When Bheem arrives, he avoids eye contact and hands his appointment slip to Riya.

The televisions are off and time slows down. I lead a bewildered ten-year-old into the treatment room and walk to the break room for a glass of water. I log on to Amazon on my phone and type *Knitting Kits for Beginners*, then change my mind and search for adult colouring books. I choose one with sketches of cats in steampunk costumes. After that I go onto the ASPCA website to look at actual cats to adopt.

I ignore his text messages that night, but at 3 a.m. he comes over unannounced and asks me to hold him. He doesn't want to have sex or undress, he says. I comply with his wish.

When I ask about his day, he gets up and avoids my gaze. He walks over to my bookshelf and picks out *Anna Karenina*.

'Do you like Tolstoy?' I ask.

'I have a thesis about this book,' he says, and pauses.

'Let's hear it,' I say.

'The scene where Dolly visits Anna is incredibly contrived. So much so that it has to have hidden meaning.'

'Is that your thesis?'

He returns to bed and places his head on my chest, but I'm shaking with laughter.

'My English teacher would have said your argument is based on speculative evidence.'

Suddenly, he asks me whether I know what it's like to be suffocated to death. He touches my neck as he says this, and then he asks me to step into the small storage room adjacent to my bedroom. I'm in my underwear because of the heat. Bheem shuts the door on me and turns off the lights from the outside. I await his instructions and close my eyes in the dark.

A mouse, or some mouse-like creature, scuttles across the floor. I calm myself by placing my hands between a pile of sweaters. A whisper of moths emerges and flutters towards me. I feel them against my face but don't move. Eventually, Bheem flings the door open when I've lost track of time. I follow him to the bedroom and we have sex, as usual, with him on top of me. Later, he berates me for refusing to play along. 'I wasn't aware of the game,' I say.

'We won't do anything you don't want to do,' he says. 'Just say the word.'

For a moment, I wonder whether we'd established a safe word and I simply forgot. More likely, he meant I should use another generic word like: stop, cease, refrain. I prefer the idea of a safe word like a private language: pineapple, ocean, tiger.

He shifts to the other side of the bed. I pull a blanket over him, shrouding him in embroidered green jellyfish. He softens and I mumble goodnight.

Bheem's large frame disappears beneath the blanket and a renewed sense of tenderness takes hold of me as he begins snoring. Bheem has a thyroid condition and carries himself like a skinny person in a padded flesh costume. He knocks into furniture and squeezes through doors, almost surprised by the size of his own body, even after all these years of inhabiting it. I like the largeness of him. I take comfort in the dent his body leaves on my mattress, so unlike my own, confirming the presence of another person. I haven't merely imagined him.

During the daytime, he sends me romantic text messages or long notes about whatever is on his mind. In these lengthy messages he expresses a vulnerability that I can never sense when he arrives at my house in the night. Perhaps to be physically and emotionally present at the same time would be too much.

When Sylvia tells me she's in Bombay, I invite her to my house because I fear what she will say and how I will react in a public space. When I look her up online, she doesn't exist. Someone has thanked her in a blog post about their chapbook titled *Sparrow Heart*, but that was five years ago. I buy a digital copy but cannot make sense of the poems, which are mostly lists of misspelled street signs and menu items. No other footprint of Sylvia exists in the virtual realm.

In an email, Sylvia tells me she's named after the bird Sylvia Lugens and not the dead poet, obviously. She then apologises because ending sentences with 'obviously' makes her sound passive-aggressive. I hadn't noticed. I bake chocolate-chip banana bread in anticipation of her visit.

She arrives on time, which surprises me because she also carries herself like someone who could fall over at any moment. I feel an overwhelming fondness because we both share memories of my mother; a bond which few people would understand. I try to see the person my mother must have known once.

Sylvia carries a pink jhola studded with tiny mirrors, which she places on the dining table. 'Coffee would be great,' she says, before I can offer. She speaks in an incessant stream, anticipating my questions or perhaps defending herself against them.

'It was easy finding this place because everyone knows the building. I have not been in Bombay in a long time but this is my second time back since I moved away. Now I'm reminded why. The traffic gets so traumatising, more and more. I don't mean that, and I shouldn't use such words lightly. I had lunch at Madras Café, which was our weekend haunt during college days but one can never have enough coffee and that's perfect – thank you – no milk. One spoon of sugar. I cannot stand Splenda and I'm so glad you use the real stuff.'

She finally takes a breath and exhales onto the surface of the dark liquid cupped between her hands.

'Aloe is hiding,' I say, when I see her noticing the toys scattered on the floor. 'She's a beautiful tabby that adopted me.' I don't want Sylvia thinking I have children, neither do I want my uterus to become a topic of conversation. I busy myself with arranging slices of the banana bread on a small plate bordered with yellow flowers.

'They remind me of sunflowers, though they must be some other variety,' Sylvia says. 'I suppose I should get to the point.' Her voice sounds small and distant, as if speaking to someone else in a corner of the room.

I sit down beside her and study her eyelashes because I cannot look directly into her eyes, nor do I want to turn away. She places a sealed envelope on the table between us, in a gesture of declaration. Your choice, she seems to be saying. Instead of opening and reading the letter, I ask her to tell me what she remembers about my mother.

Sylvia smiles. 'That's a beautiful picture,' she says, pointing to a photograph of me with my mother. We're wearing matching green dresses. She slips off her shoes and crosses her legs on the chair. I sense familiarity in her demeanour, as though she contains traces of someone I've always known.

'My family is from a caste of professional mourners,' she tells me. 'My grandmothers were hired to cry and wail at funerals; to express sadness on behalf of those who couldn't. The crying has its own syntax and vocabulary. It's like music. Your father and I were childhood sweethearts but he's a brahmin and his family wouldn't allow us to get married. Eventually, he married your mother. We had all been friends in college and I remained part of their lives. We had our ups and downs, but your mother started calling me quite often in the days before the accident. She told me the structure of the building you were all living in was unsafe. She tried bringing it up to the building committee, but no one listened because she insisted she knew everything from a prophetic dream. I was sceptical too, but sometimes we know things and forget how we know them. They just cling to our unconscious.'

'What's in the envelope?' I ask.

'Your mother was tied up in something complicated. She worked as an accountant for the contractors who owned the building your family lived in. She sent me these documents for safe-keeping. There's proof that the contractors benefited from the collapse. Take your time,' Sylvia says.

A few days later, Bheem and I decide to take the bus to Lonavala because his car broke down and we've already booked a villa for the weekend. I'm tired of meeting in my apartment late at night and Bheem insists we can't be seen together anywhere in Bombay because of his family. I could become a target, he insists. I'm beginning to believe him. Without knowing why, I carry a bottle of sedatives Dr Nisha once gave me when I complained about recurring nightmares. 'Crush half a pill and consume with milk,' she instructed. I wonder about the effects of an entire pill, or a crushed up handful. It would take a lot to knock Bheem out.

On the way to Lonavala, he squints at the street signs while I admire the light grey stubble that shades his sharp jaw, and the birthmark behind his earlobe. 'That's my most androgynous area,' he said, the first time we kissed.

'You mean erogenous,' I said, trying not to laugh.

'If you know what I mean, then why do you correct me?'

The billboards on the highway leading to Lonavala all promise marital bliss. A wedding destination for city folks who want to breathe clean air for a few hours before the wedding pyre.

'Lucky's Celebrity Wax Museum,' Bheem reads from a sign painted in large blue letters. He holds a thermos of coffee in his right hand and clasps my hand with his left. Whenever he wants to point something out, he pulls my hand with his, towards the window, refusing to let go. 'Why do they have so many wax museums,' he says.

'Do you think Lucky is actually a lucky man?'

'What's the story behind your name?'

'My parents named me Tani after a mythological woman whose voice could put out fires with its sweetness. I think they wanted me to be a singer, but I have an untrained ear. I can't distinguish one raag from another, let alone carry a tune. I prefer to be called by any other name.'

The bus comes to a stop in standstill traffic. Street vendors approach us through the windows, offering tea and chikki. Two feet away, a faulty electrical wire lets off sparks, but no one seems concerned about the fire that could ignite at any moment. Bheem places an arm around my shoulders and I feel a steady warmth, like candlelight.

I left Sylvia's envelope back at home on my bedside table, but the secrets it revealed were enclosed within me. I am afraid they'll dissolve my insides like acid if I don't move, don't do something. Bheem wants to get off the bus and stretch his legs. I offer to keep his thermos in my purse while we walk. Bheem suggests a visit to Lucky's museum.

'Fate, I've always believed, favours the impulsive,' I tell him.

The wax museum is empty except for the cashier, and us. He sells us our tickets and asks me to leave my purse with him but I refuse. 'It has important feminine items,' I say in a high-pitched voice. He gives Bheem a flustered look, hoping for support, but Bheem shrugs. Eventually, the cashier gives up and follows us inside, keeping a close eye on us.

There are three rooms: Bollywood, Hollywood and Sports. I know this from the signs, but cannot recognise any of the wax replicas. The wax women look like plasticised porn stars, but the satire isn't intentional. Eventually, the cashier loses interest and returns to his cubby. We're free to touch the wax celebrities. I'm too spooked, but Bheem puts his arm around fake Sushmita Sen's waist, then places his head against her breast like a child.

For a while I assumed Bheem didn't have a mother because he never mentioned her. He talked about his father, but mostly in arbitrary conversations about shellfish allergies or his inherited love for old Bollywood songs. I had projected onto Bheem a motherless childhood similar to mine, and perhaps I wasn't wrong. When he finally told me about his mother a few days ago, he said, 'My mother celebrated her fifty-ninth birthday today. She's bedridden with her depression.'

I remained quiet, but wondered about the grammatical accuracy of his sentence. I've been accused of distancing myself from experiences by focusing on good grammar, but I disagree.

'What about your mother?' he had asked.

'She died when I was young. We lived in an old building, which collapsed. I think Borla Constructors owned the property, or maybe they own it now. Isn't that your family's company? She worked for them, but you must have been barely a teenager back then. I don't know much about her because my father doesn't like dredging up the past.'

Bheem didn't flinch. He leaned in, undid my hair-tie and said, 'I like you with your hair down.'

'Smile please,' I say now, and take a photograph of Bheem posing with fake Shah Rukh Khan. I'm aware we won't stay together past this weekend; he is like an infected tooth that needs extracting.

ENTOMOLOGY

Professor Rao entered the classroom and slammed a pile of textbooks onto the table. Even though it was halfway through the semester, she still announced the name of the seminar after the morning bell.

'Insect Control and Toxicology,' she said in her high-pitched yet oddly sturdy voice. 'You are all expected to memorise the pain scale for your final exam. No multiple choice. All comprehension.' She paused and looked around the room like a magician about to unveil her next trick.

'Miss, will you give grace marks?' someone asked from the back corner.

'No. You're all seniors now. What grace marks? Open your books to page two hundred and twenty-nine. Someone read.'

Zena glanced at the skeletal system illustrated in her entomology textbook. *Mandible, thorax, petiole, wings and stinger.* Did paper wasps experience consciousness as a stream or as a series of ruptured sensations? Why had she chosen biology as her major?

'The tarantula spider's bite is exponentially more painful than being stung by a bee. However, damage and pain are separate categories.' Zena didn't recognise the voice. *Life is all about choices,* she wrote in the margin. She enjoyed some varieties of pain.

'The insect-sting pain scale was created by a man named Justin Shuh-mid,' the voice continued. Zena looked at the picture of him printed in the book.

'Ma'am, why is pain always measured by the experiences of men?' a woman sitting at the front of the classroom asked.

'Quiet down,' Rao said, anticipating the flurry of chatter this comment would cause. She told the voice to keep reading.

There were rumours about Professor Rao. That she was vice-principal Thampi's ex-wife. That she was the reason vice-principal Thampi had nine fingers. That she ate non-vegetarian food three times a day, including beef. That she had a scar on her ring finger from soldering off her wedding band with a crème brulee torch on the day of her divorce. From their desks, ten feet away from her lectern, students were unable to see the scar. Zena remained in awe of Rao's ability to work the rumours in her favour: classrooms hushed when she entered.

Once, during an exam, Rao placed a palm on Zena's desk. The gesture made Zena's heart race, even though she hadn't done anything wrong. She would never pass a lie detector test. Authority figures made her body switch into flight mode. Rao's fingers, Zena had noted, were devoid of scars.

After class, Zena took a rickshaw to Lek's house. She continued flipping through the textbook and imagined a pain scale for everyday catastrophes like stubbing your toe and getting scratched by an outdoor cat. The insect-sting scale didn't take into account how pain gets magnified on days when you get a bad haircut or accidentally break your favourite coffee mug or get dumped and feel doubly stung.

Two years ago, Zena had fallen for an older man who took her to a dive bar in Thane on their first date. At the bar, a stranger tried to flirt with her, and her date beat him unconscious. When they kissed later that night, she could smell the stranger's blood on him, and she tried not to flinch. Their relationship lasted five months. He was gentle with her, but every moment felt like a tightrope, tense with the events of that first night. Zena never took him to her place, and he never questioned it. When they broke up, she changed her phone number.

Since then, she had lost her ability to feel aroused by men, until she met Lokesh, whom she called Lek for unknown reasons. He had long hair up to his shoulders, and wore a green sports headband that always looked stained with sweat. She fantasised about throwing it away in a wifely gesture, but they had been together for only six months. She would have to wait until month nine.

Zena used her key to open the door to Lek's apartment. He lay on the living-room sofa with his laptop on his belly, fingers manically pressing down on the keyboard. 'I found a video game about ecological activism,' he said. 'There's a giant thunderbird. Look at this. And before I forget – I'm going to need the house-key back temporarily because Raj lost his.'

Her stomach dropped, and the cold metal key burned against her fingers as she handed it over. Red fire ants crawled up her sides. 'Do you want to have sex?' she asked.

'Let me just complete this level,' Lek said.

They went into his bedroom and Zena sat at the edge of the bed while Lek rummaged for condoms. The sex had got monotonous ever since Zena refused to spank Lek with the paddle he'd bought as a surprise. He wanted her to be cruel, but she found his request paradoxical. How can you be a sub and still be so demanding, she reasoned.

'Do you still have the paddle,' Zena said. 'I'd like to try it out.'

'Bottom drawer on your left.'

Zena took the paddle out of its clear plastic wrapping and slapped it lightly against her left palm. She wondered about the relationship between pain and intimacy. 'Use it on me,' she said.

Lek avoided eye contact but walked over to her, and she handed him the paddle. Without speaking, she got on the floor on her hands and knees, and noticed a mass of spider webs underneath the bed. She made a mental note to mention this to Lek after they were done.

'I don't really want to,' Lek said. 'I'm going to make some noodles. Do you want some?' He walked out of the room before she could lift herself off the floor.

A few days later, he broke up with her in a text message.

Zena stopped going to class, turned off her cellphone, and stayed in bed in Lek's grey T-shirt. She watched, on repeat, the same five episodes of *Broadchurch* they had seen together – refusing, out of superstition, to watch any further. She downloaded the video game about a thunderbird destroying oil pipelines and tried to imagine the pleasure Lek felt when he played it. She chewed her fingernails until she was biting skin, but felt none of the buzz she experienced when Lek grazed her skin with his teeth. There was, she realised, a period of waiting after the end of a relationship which mirrored the waiting at the beginning.

Once, she mustered enough energy to change into regular clothes and decided to make a list of reasons why she shouldn't miss Lek. She grabbed a yellow legal pad from the stack she kept in her desk drawer, and in large block letters she scrawled the word *INATTENTIVE*, followed by a question mark. What counted as listening to someone or noticing things about them? Lek always noticed when she wore a new item of clothing, but he never complimented her. 'Is this new?' he would ask, then said nothing more after her response. She crossed out inattentive and wrote down: *WITHOLDING*.

Eventually, Zena tapped into something that was part-brokenness, part-bravery and logged onto Facebook. She checked Lek's profile, bracing herself for pictures of his new girlfriend. She hadn't expected the rush of desire she felt, which almost edged out her jealousy. Lek's new girlfriend worked as a hairdresser.

Zena had once taken a class on the ethnography of emotion. She spent weeks trying to understand cruel optimism and fell behind on all her homework. Finally, a classmate told her that cruel optimism wasn't produced by the object of desire but by the act of desiring. Zena turned on her cellphone for the first time in nine days and called Happy Thoughts Hair Salon. 'Could I make an appointment for a women's cut,' she said to the voice that answered the phone. 'What days is Mona available?'

The hairdresser's height was accentuated by the fact that Zena was seated. Mona wore sparkly gold sneakers, and Zena could imagine Lek saying, 'swag'. Zena wanted to appear dramatic. She wanted to touch Mona's face, the same way Lek used to touch her after they had sex.

'I want a pixie cut,' she said. 'Can you make it look like yours?'

The question elicited the reaction Zena had wanted. Mona's eyebrows went up, and she smiled like a child discovering that her new toy is edible. 'Are you sure?' she asked. 'Are you really sure?'

Zena nodded.

Mona ran her fingers through Zena's frizzy, shoulder-length hair. She asked Zena to close her eyes and sprayed a sweet-smelling mist over her scalp. Janelle Monáe's *ArchAndroid* played over the sounds of snipping and hairdryers. Mona hummed as she cut Zena's hair with steady intensity.

'When is your birthday?' Zena asked.

Mona paused in order to answer the question. 'July,' she said. 'July twelfth.'

'You're a water sign,' Zena said, but Mona had resumed cutting and didn't hear.

Zena flipped through a fashion magazine, unable to gauge whether the silence was comfortable, strained or necessary. She came across an article that said women develop crushes on people they want to emulate. Mona seemed like a firm and nurturing person. They didn't speak for the next thirty minutes and Zena tipped twenty per cent before leaving. She felt smitten, but didn't know why.

Zena frequently fell in love with women, but told herself it was mimetic desire. A boy with hairless arms and soft lips had once read to her about Girard's double bind. He graduated from the philosophy programme and left the city soon after. Occasionally, Zena received cryptic postcards from him, with lines from surrealist poets. Their separation had been a matter of logistics: he was never returning to Bombay.

'There's no way we won't meet again,' he'd said.

When he left, Zena felt like a sixteen-year-old after a summer romance. It was a bittersweet emotion which she wallowed in for weeks, secretly pleased that she could still fall in love like a hormonal teenager. The feeling she held for Lek was different – it made her nauseous, like her internal organs were being squished together.

Zena started attending class again and got her hair styled by Mona every few weeks until it almost felt genuine: the affection she felt for this tall, ebullient woman. Months passed and Zena nearly forgot what had brought her to Mona in the first place. Being single felt easy and her pixie haircut provided an aura of sexual ambiguity that prevented nosy relatives from asking questions about her love life. Even her fantasy life was almost devoid of Lek, though sometimes she thought about Mona.

On New Year's Eve, Zena had an appointment for a trim. She wondered why Mona looked overjoyed. 'Any big plans?' Zena asked.

'Big plans?'

'For tonight.'

'For tonight, of course. I mean, of course that's what you meant. Just a night in with my boyfriend watching *Big Boss*. We just found out that we're pregnant.'

Zena smiled and nodded, afraid that her voice wouldn't work if she tried to speak.

'Thank – I mean, sorry,' Mona said, and blushed when she realised Zena hadn't congratulated her. She avoided Zena's eyes in the mirror and they lapsed into their usual silence.

It had been months since Zena had sex, or even the promise of sex. She wondered whether Lek and Mona had boring sex now that Mona was pregnant. She wondered whether they had sex at all. Zena wanted to feel close to Mona, or perhaps she wanted to maintain her closeness to Lek by proxy. She hoped Mona was more cordial with her other clients, and tried to think of ways to confirm this wishful hunch.

The salon could only fit seven people at a time, and clients who arrived early could be seen standing outside the glass entrance doors smoking cigarettes or nursing cups from the coffee shop next door. There were two chairs between the three hairstylists, one hair-washing station, and a small desk where the receptionist took payments. She would arrive early next time, Zena decided, and squeeze herself inside the salon to eavesdrop on Mona.

The following month, Zena showed up an hour early for her 4 p.m. appointment. She'd once heard a psychology student say that masochists are always early. She thought about how Lek woke up at six in the morning, and wondered whether being an early-morning person was the same as being an early person. Like a human alarm clock, he used to wake her at precisely five minutes to seven.

Zena stood awkwardly between the door and the reception desk, and caught snippets of conversation between the sound of hairdryers and running water. Was Mona inviting this client to her baby shower? Or was she trying to explain how being pregnant made it difficult to shower? That couldn't be true, Zena thought.

'Do you have any ibuprofen,' Zena asked the receptionist.

'No, would you like to take a seat?'

There were no chairs available, so Zena just smiled and shook her head. Telling someone you wouldn't like to take a seat felt too aggressive. 'Nice nail art,' she said.

The receptionist brightened. 'Mona did it for me.'

Zena felt a cramp and wondered whether she was about to get her period. She imagined the humiliation of bleeding all over the chair while having her hair styled. Lost in the possibility of this scenario, Zena missed the rest of Mona's conversation with the client who had been invited to the baby shower. She took solace in the way Mona beamed when she saw Zena waiting.

Halfway through the haircut, right when Mona's scissors were poised to snip, Zena saw Lek in the mirror. She turned her head abruptly and the scissors nicked her behind the ear. Mona gasped and started apologising, even though it had been Zena's fault. A first-aid kit was brought. Everyone stopped working and gathered around them. Lek stood near the door and Zena avoided his gaze. Maybe he wouldn't recognise her, she thought. Mona applied an unnecessary amount of Dettol to the cut and Zena felt a pleasurable sting from the antiseptic. She wondered whether some varieties of pain felt good because of the anticipation of after-care. Seeing that the damage was minimal, everyone went back to their stations, and Lek walked over to greet Mona. He kissed her on the cheek and nodded at Zena in a non-committal manner.

'I won't charge for the haircut,' Mona said.

'Your hair looks different,' Lek said.

'You two know each other,' Mona said.

Zena remained silent. She wanted to fall into Mona's arms and sob. She wanted Mona to break Lek's heart in solidarity with her. Where was Mona on the spectrum of feminism, she wondered, losing track of the conversation between Mona and Lek.

'You're good to go,' Mona said, tapping Zena on the shoulder. 'And we'll see you for dinner tonight. Lek has your number.'

On her way home, Zena tried to remember what had been said. How much did Mona know? How did Lek feel about her? Why had they asked her to dinner? Insisted, even. She floated home, showered, changed and called an Uber, which dropped her outside Lek's apartment. At the door to his house, she realised her mistake and texted Lek to say she would be late. They were meeting at Mona's place, which was in the opposite direction.

Lek opened the door to Mona's place when Zena arrived.

'Are you like, living together now,' she said.

'You're on time for once,' Lek said, and squeezed her shoulder but didn't hug her.

Zena followed him past the living room and into the kitchen. Mona was stirring a pot of red basil curry and gestured for Lek to carry a bowl of rice into the dining area. Their movements in the kitchen were graceful and coordinated, as if they had rehearsed this scene many times.

'Hope you like Thai food,' Mona said.

'You made all this?'

'Wouldn't that be something? No, the maid cooked. I'm just heating it up. I sent her to Deepak Cinema. It's one of the last few single-screen cinemas around. She refuses to go to the multiplexes. It overwhelms her and the ushers are rude.'

'Can I help with anything?'

'Make yourself at home,' Mona said.

Zena wasn't sure whether she should make herself at home in the living room or in the dining room where Lek was setting the table. She felt like an audience member who has been invited onstage without clear instructions. Unable to decide, she lingered in the kitchen and feigned interest in the magnetic poetry on the fridge.

Naked nasty thighs/ tremendous trembling caress/ & a murmur. These two, Zena concluded, were not particularly skilled as poets.

During dinner, Lek told a story that Zena remembered differently, but she didn't correct him. 'On our first date,' Lek said, 'I pretended to live in Bandra, just so I could share a taxi with Zee and spend a few more minutes with her. We started making out, and the driver started coughing to get us to stop, but we just ignored him completely. She was wearing this dark maroon lipstick, and when I finally got home my roommates started giggling because my lips were stained with colour. So, next time, I got my revenge and gave her a love bite.'

Every first kiss begins with an invocation: a hand reaching for another hand, a tilt of the head or a gaze that lingers. Lek had leaned forward and touched the tip of her nose with his finger before kissing her. It had been, Zena remembered, in a parking lot outside a café after their first date. But did any of that matter, as long as he recalled their first kiss with fondness? Even if it was overlaid with the ordinary details of his experience with some other woman.

'How cute,' Mona said.

No one said anything for a few moments. The dining table was adjacent to a small balcony with a glass sliding door and red batik curtains that were drawn open. Mona's apartment was on the second floor and there wasn't much to see except the neighbouring apartment where a middle-aged couple watched television while eating bowls of fruit. 'They always look content, those two,' Mona said, breaking the silence that had settled over them. 'In the afternoons she gives sitar lessons to other women in the building. He's always home for dinner. Watching them is very soothing.'

Lek drank too many glasses of red wine and Mona spooned too much ice cream onto her slice of pie. Zena wondered what her own excess was that evening and what anxieties it revealed. Had she talked too much? Things were pleasant enough: the couple behaved graciously, expressed interest in Zena's work, and didn't make her feel excluded. Living together without getting married had been a romantic decision, they told her – choosing to be with each other every day without a binding contract. This wasn't the same man she had dated. The man who once pretended to have lost the five-page handwritten letter she gave him because he didn't want to acknowledge her confession of love.

Eventually, the three of them moved to the living room and kept drinking. Mona and Zena sat next to each other and Lek placed himself in the armchair across from them.

'He called me by your name once,' Mona said. She was addressing Zena, but her eyes were on Lek.

'What,' Zena said.

'Zee,' Mona said. 'During sex. He called me by your name. I thought I had imagined it. You have such a unique name. And then you started coming to the salon.'

'You knew who I was,' Zena said.

'We have a guest,' Lek said, as if the conversation had nothing to do with Zena.

'I'm trying to communicate with you,' Mona said. 'If this is what it takes, then, well, I don't know.'

Zena rubbed Mona's shoulder and said, 'There there. All this sadness, it's bad for the baby.'

'You're getting hysterical,' Lek said.

'Why don't you just listen to her,' Zena said. 'Try to acknowledge her pain.'

'What are you even doing here?' Lek said, his face turning red. 'You don't even know what this is about.'

'He makes everything about him, when I try to explain how I'm feeling. He doesn't get it. He thinks I don't feel trapped by this situation. I had money saved up to start my own business, and now what?'

Suddenly Mona leaned forward and her left hand gripped Lek's hair. For a moment, Zena thought it was a gesture of affection. She noticed Lek's face scrunch up, and realised Mona had pulled a few strands of hair from his scalp. Mona proceeded to slap his arms until he grabbed her wrists to restrain her.

How did Mona move with such agility, Zena wanted to ask. Instead, she got up from the couch and said, 'I'll call an Uber.' She had once watched a video where a relationship therapist said couples should use touch to express love when words failed them.

'Why don't you hug her,' she said to Lek, who was picking up the used wineglasses. Mona had her face between her palms. Zena moved towards the door.

'Stay,' Mona stated firmly. Lek's face remained neutral at this pronouncement, but he put the glasses back on the coffee table and sat down next to Mona. He placed an arm around her and glanced at Zena, indicating that she should leave.

Zena felt an urge to sink to the ground right where she stood. In her mind she calculated the proportion of food to alcohol she had consumed that evening. Not enough carbs, she reminded herself. She looked at Lek, whose eyes were bloodshot, either from the wine or from holding back tears. The thought crossed her mind that she was a bad person.

'I'll go,' she said. 'We're taking a field trip to the Aarey Milk Colony bee farm. Early morning. And I think my Uber is here.'

On the taxi ride home, Zena wondered if the entire evening had been leading up to that moment. Had she been a catalyst for their fight? Zena imagined them having make-up sex, and remembered Lek's strange, strained grunting.

'What would you be doing, if you weren't studying insects,' Lek had asked her once, as they lay in bed.

'I could have been a jewellery designer. Why do you ask?'

'I would have built furniture,' Lek said.

Zena thought of the idiom 'to stir up a hornet's nest', and how she'd once been stung by stepping on a dead wasp. It felt like pain. There were adjectives and quantifications, but no analogy for the experience of blinding physical pain. As an adolescent, the causes had always seemed so simple: bug bites, stomach aches, period cramps, playing hot hands, experimenting with cutting, accidentally stabbing yourself with a compass while trying to draw a perfect full moon. The dinner with Mona and Lek didn't register on Zena's pain scale. She felt calm, as if in anticipation of the tooth fairy or love at first sight – things she didn't fully believe in.

Zena had once known a woman who could predict the length of a relationship before it even began. At parties, they would drink whisky sours and stand in a corner watching people couple off.

'One night,' Bina would say, pointing at a man in a denim jacket with his arm around a bored-looking woman.

'Two weeks,' Zena attempted. She pointed at two men who appeared to be yelling into each other's ears.

'No,' Bina said, rolling her eyes. 'They've already been together two weeks. It's so obvious. Their smiles almost match. I give them five more months.'

Zena and Bina had drifted apart when Zena met Lek. She had been afraid to introduce the two of them. Perhaps because of Bina's superpower, or perhaps for reasons she kept hidden from herself. She always wondered whether Bina knew, whether she saw the puppy-dog adoration in Zena's eyes and knew he didn't feel the same.

The next morning, seventeen biology students arrived at Aarey Milk Colony in a rented schoolbus. The trip would conclude their unit on insect bites and venoms. Rao took a headcount as they exited the bus. Eight students had got out of it by claiming an aggressive bee-sting allergy, and one had a family function to attend. Rao introduced the group to the beekeeper who would be their tour guide.

Zena had forgotten her sunglasses on the bus and returned to retrieve them. She found Professor Rao back in her seat and asked if she was okay.

'I'm just tired,' Rao said. 'When you're my age, everything hurts. All your joints hurt, and you constantly feel like you could fall over.'

'It gets better with time doesn't really apply here,' Zena said, then regretted her words.

In the distance, the tour had commenced, and someone shrieked, followed by laughter.

'Take this,' Rao said, and pushed a warm Frooti into Zena's hand. Zena realised she looked like a suck-up, staying back to chat with the teacher. The juice pack, which she felt obliged to accept, embarrassed her like a mother's overbearing embrace.

'Go on, get going,' Rao said.

Zena remembered something Professor Rao had said, about how complicated questions can have the simplest answers. 'I liked your lecture on *Apis mellifera*,' she said. She stepped off the bus to join the others, having forgotten her sunglasses yet again, but enjoying the harsh afternoon sunlight against her skin like dozens of small biting insects.

WESTWARD

> 'I kept on thinking. If I could speak fluent English, I would ask Professor Freud at least once what his own love of dogs signified. Being a famous psychologist, what did he think about it?'
>
> – *The Westward Traveller*,
> Durgabati Ghose

Calcutta, 1931

Mrs Bose often said she did not approve of her husband's profession. She claimed she found it upsetting that Girindrasekhar Bose's patients were *supposed to* fall in love with him.

'Even the men,' she grumbled.

'It depends on the relationship with their father,' Mr Bose said in the sing-song voice reserved for his wife. He had no reason to worry because Mrs Bose was secretly relieved to share the burden of making Mr Bose feel loved and appreciated.

In fact, Mrs Bose wasn't simply jealous of the men and women who spent an hour, three times a week, on Mr Bose's lounge chair. It was also Mr Bose she envied. The smart clothes he wore, the hours he spent alone in his study writing papers about Indian family structures, and the attention he received from clients and colleagues. Her husband had founded the Indian Psychoanalytical Society, and his recent article on the inverted Oedipal triangle in Indian culture had elicited a letter from Dr Freud himself.

Giri, as friends liked to call him, spent the morning fretting. He clutched the letter opener in one hand and the unopened envelope in the other. Mrs Bose thought he looked like a nervous bride. She recalled a similar sensation in the early days of their courtship, when he sent her telegraphic notes coded with amorous intent. *I am fine and hope you are doing fine as well. Wish you the very best. Write back at soonest.*

When Giri left for his evening walk, Mrs Bose entered his study, hoping to glance through the contents of the envelope from Berggasse 19, Vienna. Seeing that it was still unopened, she held it up to the light, but the paper was too thick for her to make out any words. She sat down in the deck chair, taking in the room, which she rarely entered. The papers scattered on the desk brought her back once more to the period of their courtship and she felt a knot form in her throat, as if she were mourning an ex-lover. Across from where she sat was a small wooden armchair and the desk that had been imported from London. Two potted plants stretched their leaves toward the west window. The room was sparse. Mr Bose kept his books and trinkets in the living room because he didn't want his objects to influence the patients while they recounted their dreams.

Mrs Bose awakened from her reverie to the sound of her daughter's voice. Soraya had recently ended a vow of silence, which had been meant to please the gods so they would keep her husband in good health. She lived down the street with her husband, and she was always coming and going from her parents' house.

'What are you doing in here?' Soraya said, standing in the doorway. Mrs Bose looked at her daughter's sallow face and wondered whether she was happy. No one had ever asked Mrs Bose whether she was happy, nor was it a question she asked of herself or her only daughter. For a moment, she was very glad she didn't have a son.

Mrs Bose lifted herself from the deck chair and folded it up with an ease that belied her slight frame. She yelled for the maid to dust and sweep the room before Mr Bose returned. Then Soraya and she retired to the women's quarters for tea.

They fell into a silence. Even though Soraya's maun vrat had ended, she needed time to find her momentum, to re-enter the world of the speaking. Soraya's husband was a high-ranking civil servant who suffered from asthma. Mr Ghose (or Mr Ghost, as Giri referred to him in his absence) had particularly bad symptoms during the rainy season.

'He's feeling better?' Mrs Bose asked.

Soraya held a biscuit between her fingers but didn't bite into it. She had always been plump, but starved herself these days because it wasn't appropriate for a wife to be in better health than her husband. 'It doesn't work so fast,' she said. 'He's on a special diet now, and we have to go back again next year.'

Recently, Soraya and her husband had travelled to Hyderabad to partake in the Bathini Goud ritual. Hundreds of people attended the annual event where the Goud family dispensed medicine by making each person swallow a two-inch fish. The herbal paste that cured asthma was placed in the fish's mouth. Soraya had watched, entranced, as some people swallowed with ease while others struggled with the fish thrashing inside their closed mouth. The fish slid down her husband's throat within seconds. His breath still smelled of asfoetida, she thought.

The sound of the gate informed them of Mr Bose's arrival and Soraya went to greet him. 'So thin,' he said. 'Why so thin?'

'Have you opened the letter?' Mrs Bose asked.

Soraya was having trouble keeping up with the speed of regular conversation, but nodded each time her mother spoke.

'No, but look.' He produced a small piece of paper with a man's face drawn on it, and slipped it into Soraya's hand with the subtlety of a schoolgirl passing love notes in class. 'I met Jitendra on the walk. He drew *this*.'

'What is it?' Mrs Bose asked.

'Professor Freud,' Mr Bose said. He couldn't contain his excitement, but the women returned to their tea.

'Jitendra has never seen Freud. He drew a portrait from a dream,' Bose said, trying to win back their attention, but they were out of earshot.

Soraya raised her eyebrows at her mother, who simply shook her head. 'And what other news?' her mother said. Mrs Bose had encouraged Soraya to visit a gynaecologist, though Soraya considered it a form of bullying. Women lose their power if they don't have babies, Mrs Bose had reminded her. This remained true despite Mr Ghose's subdued nature. No longer having an excuse to avoid the question, Soraya shrugged and shook her head.

'No news. He told me, if I have the money, there's a doctor in Europe. I should go soon.'

Mr Bose had opened the envelope and was pacing in the living room. 'He read my paper,' Mr Bose said to no one in particular. 'He wants me to write to Ernest Jones and get membership to the International Psychoanalytical Society. He doesn't agree with my theory,' Mr Bose added, perhaps for the benefit of his grandfather's ghost, who was said to haunt the courtyard.

Soraya took her leave and left her parents to bicker. Her husband would be waiting in his innocuous manner, which infuriated her. He rarely visited the Boses at their home and Soraya's in-laws kept a cordial distance from her and her parents. Soraya tried to push her anger aside. The unspeakable rumours about her father's work were exponentially worse than the reality. And yet, defending her father to outsiders would mean passing on to her future children a legacy of unbelonging. They too would be ostracised in small ways.

Despite being named after a fierce goddess, Soraya never expressed her fury to anyone. Once a week, she scrubbed her skin with sugar wax to rid her body of hair. She did this with unnecessary force, as if cleansing herself of undesirable emotions. Often, she watched her sister-in-law, who held herself with such grace, and longed to know the secret to perfection.

Would her father call this repression? Soraya wondered. As a teenager, she had snuck into his study and read through his notebooks. He kept extensive documentation on each of his patients. Their stories were sad, and often erotic.

Soraya's knowledge of sex had come from the narratives of her father's patients. Most of them were upper-class Bengali or Anglo-Indian men. There was one woman, the wife of a company man from London. At first, she had reported experiencing unbearable jealousy because her husband regularly called upon a known courtesan. Eventually, she revealed her own dreams of sexual encounters with the courtesan.

One of Mr Bose's patients had been a railway signal controller. His supervisor made him go into analysis because the young signalman had been experiencing constant déjà vu. In the resulting confusion, he didn't know when to signal. Hadn't a train just passed by? he thought. Was he imagining the approaching train? *Patient associates oncoming train with premature ejaculation*, Mr Bose reported in his notebook. It was after marriage, and through conversations with her sister-in-law, that Soraya learned the meaning of that phrase.

Mr Ghose's inexpressivity was a force in itself. The opposite of a ghost, Soraya thought – a body without any of its attached emotions. She had seen him weep once, while reading a book about birds. Had she imagined it? When Mr Ghose came inside her, Soraya watched his face with wonder and curiosity. He closed his eyes and pursed his lips, as if annoyed. Soraya would imagine the railway signalman and what it must feel like when a train is always arriving.

When she returned home, Soraya was surprised to find Mr Ghose looking excited. 'Our travel documents have arrived,' he said. Their trip to Europe was organised by Thomas Cook. They would take the train to Bombay in three weeks. Beneath the overwhelming irritation Mr Ghose evoked in Soraya, there existed a deep attachment. An almost-affection built on a mutual loneliness and a shared desire to travel. They were pleasant to each other and would prove to be good travel companions.

Soraya felt least annoyed with him in the mornings, when they drank their tea in silence. Occasionally, Mr Ghose would read newspaper headlines out loud and Soraya nodded or clicked her tongue. *Calcutta Policeman Shot. Frontier Raids. Newspaper Copies Seized. Exhorting to Rebellion. Allegations Against the Police. Protest Against High Cost of Rice.*

In preparation for their travels, Mr Ghose started reading to her from a novel about British society. The novel had been banned for obscenity and Mr Ghose would censor those sections when he read to Soraya. He would purse his lips and remain silent while his eyes skimmed the page, searching for the next scene. Soraya didn't mind. She no longer cared for the grand novels of her father's bookshelves, which revealed a spectrum of experiences from joy to heartache. Most days, she felt irritated and slightly betrayed by the lies of D.H. Lawrence.

Mrs Bose insisted on unfolding and re-folding every item of clothing Soraya placed in her suitcase. They were leaving the next day. Mr Bose and Mr Ghose were conversing in the veranda. Soraya's husband would be cheerful after her parents left. This always happened when he spent time with them. Soraya wasn't sure whether he took pleasure in their visit or their departure.

'Stop doing that,' Soraya said to her mother in Bengali.

'I went to New Market and got you these bangles. Don't pack them, they'll break. Just wear them. And guess who I met at the market? Enid and her new boyfriend. Even though she knows about his wife.' Mrs Bose's arms moved with manic energy when she gossiped.

'Stay out of it.'

'I'm just telling you what I saw. And this is the letter of introduction from your father, don't forget.'

That night, Soraya barely slept. In her mind, she made a list of things she would do in the morning, before they left home. Make tea, send the maid to buy bread and apples, lock all the rooms, leave a set of keys with the neighbour, scatter grain for the pigeons one last time.

She slept facing away from Mr Ghose. Sometimes she imagined the warm body beside her belonged to someone else. A man she had fallen in love with as a teenager, who wrote love letters and held her hand when no one was looking. Other times she imagined a small child's body in the space between them. Soraya had never fallen in love with Mr Ghose, but she knew he would make a good father and she clung to this hope.

Vienna, 1931

On their first morning in Vienna, Soraya ventured out with a map and the letter from her father. Mr Ghose had made plans to have lunch with a Bengali gentleman they had befriended during their travels. He had shared their railway compartment from Paris to Vienna and told the couple his family history. He told them everything, beginning with his grandfather's tailor shop being burned down by dacoits and how his nephew worked at the Taj Mahal restaurant in New York. Liquor wasn't allowed in America, he informed them. His nephew made money selling a home-brew which the Bengali gentleman had given him the recipe for. Soraya had watched her husband's face while the gentleman told these stories, curious to know whether he approved or disapproved, but Mr Ghose appeared unmoved. When the gentleman made a crude joke, Mr Ghose nodded in acknowledgement. It struck Soraya that she never saw her husband laugh, at least not in the way she laughed with her childhood friends – the kind of laughter where your body responds and you're surprised by your own delight.

A man sweeping his yard had been staring at Soraya. She asked whether he knew Professor Freud, and he pointed at a neighbouring house, continuing to stare as she proceeded up the pathway. A woman answered the door and led Soraya into the parlour without asking questions.

Freud entered the room a few minutes later, trailing the scent of cigar smoke. Soraya handed him the letter from her father.

'Your father's work,' Freud said. 'I find it interesting. Please, let's talk in my study.'

Soraya sat on an upholstered armchair in the centre of the room and wondered whether she could convince her father to get one too. It would never survive the humidity in Calcutta, she decided. Freud looked nothing like the portrait Jitendra Babu had drawn. He looked frail as he fumbled with a letter opener.

A German shepherd sauntered into the room and sniffed Soraya's feet, then placed his front paws on her lap and offered his head for scratching. 'Please call the dog away,' Soraya said, trying to maintain her composure. She preferred cats because they killed mice and cockroaches. Dogs were simply another mouth to feed.

'Wolf,' Freud said, and whistled. The dog walked towards Freud's desk and wagged his tail. Freud smiled, as if a secret had been uncovered. 'Wolf is harmless. He bit Ernest Jones once, but the doctor deserved it.'

Soraya decided her best option for a quick exit was to remain silent. She stood up and indicated her intention to leave.

At the door, Freud asked where she was staying. 'My daughter will pick you up from your hotel and show you around tomorrow. I'm afraid I won't have the time. Give your father my best. Ask him,' he added, 'what your fear of dogs might indicate.'

Without saying anything in response, Soraya turned around and walked off. She realised she was going in the wrong direction, but her husband wasn't expecting her back at the hotel for another two hours. After walking briskly for twenty minutes, she entered a café.

Mr Ghose was always in a rush to sit down and never took the time to consider which table might offer the most advantageous view. Alone for the first time, Soraya paused to consider her options. She chose a table by the window, next to two women who were reading in silence, three tables away from the ruckus of the four young men dressed in suits.

The waiter spoke loudly in stilted English, which caught the attention of the two women. Every so often they would glance at Soraya, who wore a silk blue sari. The peacock blue stood out against the muted colours of everyone else. One woman wore an olive-green dress while the other wore a pleated brown skirt with a checked shirt. Soraya pointed at the cups the women were drinking from.

'Piccolo,' the waiter said, as if announcing the name of a favourite child.

She nodded and said, 'Thank you.'

He studied her face and then vanished, returning a few minutes later with her coffee and a glass of water.

One woman smiled, held up a cup towards Soraya and said, 'Gandhi!' The second woman offered Soraya a cigarette.

Soraya declined the cigarette. They returned to reading their books. Gandhi was in prison, and had been a frequent topic of conversation during her travels through Europe. Usually her husband led the discussion and she nodded along. What would she say to these women if her English were better? Soraya wondered. They had darker skin and hair, like the women she had seen in Italy. Perhaps they were from elsewhere.

On her way back to Hospiz Rosauernante, Soraya stopped by the Thomas Cook office to pick up the mail and send a letter to her parents. For once, she had the freedom to write her innermost feelings without Mr Ghose reading over her shoulder. The physical distance made her feel bold enough to write with candour.

I cannot wait to return home. The food here is bland and I am tired of boiled vegetables and rice. I have a new appreciation for the small pleasures of home, and your mutton curry. Is it wrong to be in a sour mood? I have seen the pyramids of Egypt and the famous floral clocks of Switzerland, but I long for familiar faces. Yesterday, I went to the doctor because I had a toothache. I also visited Professor Freud, who sends his regards.

After mailing the letter, Soraya stopped at a church across the street from the hotel. Her husband would be at lunch still. Soraya sat down at a pew and watched a woman in a dark green dress enter the confessional. It looked like the cabinet magicians used, she thought. Fifteen minutes later, the woman emerged. Soraya tried to gauge whether she looked transformed, but the woman hurried off before any kind of telepathy could take place between them. Her father always said nothing is ever truly secret.

Walking into the large, empty dining room, Soraya prepared herself to once again step into the role of dutiful wife. Her husband and the Bengali gentleman were drinking tea. Their smiles looked so similar, she thought, as they greeted her. She didn't smile. They would interpret it as a sign of demureness. 'I'll go take a bath and change my clothes,' she said to Mr Ghose and retired to their room.

LUMINOUS

I grew up in Jaipur and moved to Delhi after completing a master's in linguistics. I graduated top of my class at Jaipur University and was recruited to join the Future Wreckage Committee. There were originally twelve of us in the FWC. Newly graduated linguists, environmental scientists, policy specialists, and even an eco-poet. Our task was to gauge the effects of the new light, which was still an intermittent phenomenon. We were also to create a document of recommendations and warnings for future generations. My role was to ensure the language of our document remained translatable across centuries. This requirement, along with the poet's inclusion in our committee, felt ominous. One resorts to poetry when all else fails.

The poet, whose name was Susan, read an original poem at each weekly meeting. She remained silent and took notes the rest of the time. We met for three hours every Friday, and were otherwise isolated from each other in our labs and offices. Susan's poems usually lamented the loss of something or the other: an elephant species, a dialect from South India, reproductive rights, attention spans, raw cane sugar in cola drinks. Those poems worked word-magic during our meetings. The presentations, even with their data-heavy bar graphs, were imbued with melancholy.

Just once, Susan read a poem that wasn't her own. It was by the nineteenth-century poet Emily Dickinson: *Love is the Fellow of the Resurrection / Scooping up the Dust and chanting 'Live'!*

A few weeks into the programme, Susan invited me over for coffee. Since we are the only two women on the committee, it makes sense, her email invitation said. All twelve of us had been given apartments in the same housing complex. Susan lived in the east wing of the building while I was in the north wing. I walked over to her place on a Friday evening with a box of homemade chocolate biscotti.

Susan had an aura of perfection. Apart from the plain dresses she wore, she reminded me of high society women who get photographed just for eating at restaurants or visiting playgrounds with their children. She always knew what to say, and moved around a room with the grace of someone who had practiced walking with books balanced on their head. Even her hugs had an engineered precision; they felt welcoming without being suffocating.

When I entered her apartment, the jars were the first thing I noticed. Her windowsills were lined with glass jars filled with flower buds floating in a transparent liquid. 'They soak in the sunlight,' she explained. The jars were unlabelled, but she recited their names for me like a healing prayer: chrysanthemum, frangipani, jasmine, elderflower, rose. 'Rosewater isn't so much a remedy as it is an aphrodisiac,' she added.

'Have you studied the effects of the new light on these remedies?' I asked.

'Not really,' she said.

Susan gestured for me to follow her into the kitchen. She pulled a large journal from a shelf of recipe books and handed it to me. 'That's my great-great-grandmother's recipe book, but it also contains all these medicinal potions, and life advice. My grandma and my mother added their own notes. Will you have coffee or tea? Please sit down.'

I flipped through the book while Susan boiled water for tea. The first page said *Connecticut, 1876*.

'I grew up in Connecticut and went to college in Amherst. This is my first time living somewhere that isn't New England.'

'You've adjusted quite well,' I said. 'Sorry, I'm not being very attentive. This book is captivating. It should be in a library. The penmanship is stunning.'

'One of those recipes is for a brew that cures irregular periods, but it's actually intended to induce an abortion. There're all these secrets in there, I haven't figured them all out.'

Susan wanted to know where I grew up and whether I was close to my family. 'I'm not myself around my mother,' I said. 'Or you could say I'm *too much* myself around her. I tend to regress and turn into a sixteen-year-old. I don't know why I'm stuck at that particular age in my relationship with her. Does that ever happen to you with some people? Everything is frozen at some point in time and returning to them, talking to them, is like travelling into the past.'

'Or travelling into the future? I once dated a woman who made me feel like I was seventy. It felt as if I'd spent a lifetime with her, even though our relationship, in reality, lasted two weeks. I used to have these flashes, like memories that didn't exist. I would imagine her scolding our children or cooking dinner together. Domestic scenes. Maybe it meant I was falling in love.'

'Why didn't things work out?'

'She had neglected to mention that she already had a girlfriend. They'd been living together for two years. I found out after the girlfriend went through her phone and sent me a long email. Oddly, the girlfriend's message was considerate and gentle, almost apologetic.' Susan paused and looked at me as if expecting another question. I would come to learn this mannerism and wait out the silence. She was like a cat kneading a blanket, getting comfortable, opening up to me.

'This tea is lovely,' I said.

'It's a special brew. Bitter, but good for memory. According to the recipe book, it's also good for one's intuition.'

'Was it difficult?' I asked. 'Uprooting your life to move here.'

'Lydia, the woman whose girlfriend emailed me, she called me again. I hadn't heard from her in months, and then a few weeks before I leave for India, she calls. She told me she broke up with the girlfriend and that she missed me. If she'd called a few days earlier, everything might have gone differently. I still think about that. I worry I'll never stop thinking about that.'

'You didn't get a chance to get sick of each other. Everything you liked about each other would have eventually turned out to be exactly what irritated you most.'

'It sounds like you're speaking from experience. With you, I already have a feeling of presence. Like we'll always be in the now.'

Back at the office that week, I studied data collected from Google Books on words that had gone out of fashion. For my dissertation, I had looked at nineteeth-century novels that remained popular and what made them resound with contemporary audiences.

When the light first appeared, years ago, we would catch glimpses of neon-blue sun's rays refracted in glass objects like monochrome rainbows. In retrospect, I wonder why no one feared the novelty. The light got stronger over the months, allowing our eyes to adjust. The first physical symptoms were a buzzing in the ears and a tingling on the surface of the skin. Like a fever during flu season, people seemed comforted to know everyone had been experiencing the same thing. I've heard it compared to the EFT technique of tapping your cortices. The light channels, or feeds into, the energy currents running through our bodies. The chronic stimulation begins to feel like fatigue. I started imagining pieces of lint were covering the inside of my mouth. I also developed a cough.

There was a spike in demand for black-out curtains and some people avoided the light while others used it like a drug. When all our symptoms worsened, the scientists started taking notice. The first dissertation on the new light was published in 2015 by a Swedish woman who studied its effects on ant colonies. Everything became chaos, she concluded. The ants reacted to the light as though it were rain: by seeking shelter.

At the weekly meeting, there was an atmosphere of mild panic after the sleep scientists presented their findings. According to them, the new light chipped away at our capacity for the sleep phase that permits dreaming. Eventually we wouldn't sleep at all, they suggested. They were unsure how our evolution into sleepless creatures would affect life expectancy. These projections are for hundreds of years from now, they assured us.

The historian appeared unperturbed. 'In medieval times, sleeping actually put one at a disadvantage,' he said. 'While asleep, you could be more easily attacked or possessed by a ghost.'

'We still haven't confirmed whether dreams perform a necessary function,' one scientist chimed in.

Susan suggested getting a drink after the meeting. We headed to a local pub which served cocktails infused with flavours like saffron and cardamom.

'Why do you think shared sleep is such an intensely intimate experience? That's one of the things I'm most afraid of losing. Falling asleep next to someone you love,' Susan said.

As if picking up from our previous conversation, I found myself telling her about Devin, the man I'd broken up with ten months ago because I'd fallen in love with him.

'You are hilarious,' Susan said. 'Is that a cultural thing? Ending a relationship because you might actually like the other person?'

'No. It was just too strange, the way I felt about him. We slept together once, after dating for a month, but it felt like I'd known him forever. But also like I didn't know him at all. He was a really good communicator. Really made an effort to understand what made me feel safe and cared for. But I knew that would eventually drive me mad. He was too emotionally mature.'

'Well, that's very mature of you to admit,' Susan said.

'Have you noticed that the engineers no longer attend our weekly meetings? All three of them were absent today. I don't know whether they quit or were fired.'

'Does reading apocalyptic novels ever turn you on?'

'It's understandable that end-of-the-world fiction might lead to inappropriate fantasising,' I said, unsure whether the question was intended to be intellectual or flirtatious.

Artefact #18

Eye Masks. Also known as sleep masks, these were once functional devices worn over the eyes to block out residual light from traffic, streetlamps, nightlights, or even the sun. This was before the new light became capable of penetrating all materials including wood, metal and titanium. They could be used all night or for short naps in the daytime. Eye masks were available in a variety of fabrics such as cotton, silk and jersey. The masks displayed here include gel inserts that cooled the skin around the eyes and were meant for use with earplugs (See: Artefact #24).

I fell ill, and Susan took care of me. She brought murky brews for me to drink. In secret, I also took a course of antibiotics prescribed by my family doctor. The illness had nothing to do with the light, but I slept badly. Fits of coughing woke me and often ended with me retching into the small bucket by my bedside.

Susan insisted on staying with me while I recovered. She told me her great-great-grandmother had been a watcher.

'Like the watchmen?' I said, delirious from my fever.

'Like a nurse. The watcher's job was to sit by the sick person's bed and keep an eye on them. In case their illness got worse or they needed anything.'

'I'm not dying,' I said, even though I liked having Susan as my watcher. It didn't feel like surveillance.

My parents visited in January. I tried warning them by giving them a gift basket with sunscreen, umbrella hats and sunglasses. These were the only preventive measures we knew about. The sunscreen was most likely a placebo.

My parents were staying at a hotel. I took them to an Udupi restaurant for lunch. I didn't want them to see my apartment because my mother would try to re-decorate and send me unnecessary things like wind-chimes and miniature bonsai.

'SPF 2500 sounds excessive,' my mother said. 'Anyway, it's still going to be freezing in Jaipur for another two months.'

'I can take you shopping for those large parkas with hoods. I know a great place.'

'I appreciate your concern,' my mother said.

'We came to see you, not to shop,' my dad said.

The new light keeps us awake and disrupts our circadian rhythms. Cats are immune to it. Years from now, they will be the only species to survive. We were right about the engineers vanishing. My supervisor, whom I had yet to meet, sent me an email informing me that my responsibilities had expanded to include the creation of a time capsule. Her email insinuated that I should keep the contents of the capsule PG-13. A committee in charge of supervising our committee had been created and she was busy making arrangements. I would be allowed an intern.

Artefact #39

Sound loop of snoring man. Many romantic relationships suffered due to an incurable respiratory impairment that caused people to breathe noisily while asleep. Men were more frequently afflicted than women. The noise was referred to as a snore. Some snores were soft like whistles, but others resembled a power drill. In this particular recording, an unknown man snores like a tea-kettle coming to the boil.

The intern introduced himself as Prakash and asked what kind of accent I wanted him to use when answering the phone. 'I've trained for all the regions,' he said. 'I can do a Texas drawl or British Columbia, or even a hybrid like New-Jersey-with-desi-parents.'

'We don't get many phone calls,' I said.

He grinned in a way that made all his front teeth visible. 'I've never worked one of those scams. Always wanted to learn.'

'There's no scam. It's just research. I need your help with logistics, but some of it is also confidential, and we haven't run your background check yet. So I can't tell you much more for now.'

'Of course,' he said, in a soothing voice. 'Research and logistics.'

'I need you to track down Neeta Sinha and get permission for us to use her photograph of the Jantar Mantar sun dial.'

Prakash grinned again.

'It's not a scam,' I said, suspecting that he would never believe me.

The next morning Prakash sent me an email with Sinha's home address, studio address, credit card number and Aadhar information. I sent him a text asking him to come by my office. Our floor had dozens of empty cubicles, which formed a maze between the elevators and the line of east-facing offices with translucent doors.

I never knew which cubicle Prakash worked at, and found this slightly unsettling.

'What is this,' I said, when he entered my office.

'Did you want the passport number as well?' Prakash was tall and never seemed to know what to do with the length of his arms. His hands clutched his elbows in a manner that made him appear defensive.

Artefact #72

Worry Dolls. These two-inch wool dolls were used to ward off nightmares and soothe anxious children. The dreamer would tell the doll their worries before bedtime and sleep with it under their pillow. Sometimes multiple dolls were used for an excess of anxieties. In the morning, the dreamer's worries would have vanished because the dolls took them away at night.

'Can you explain to me why you're still collecting credit card numbers,' I asked Prakash, but didn't receive an answer because the fire alarm went off. We took the stairs to the ground floor and stood outside in the torrid afternoon heat. Sweaty and pre-emptively nostalgic for natural sunlight, I asked Prakash about his childhood. He spoke about growing up on a farm, and raising emus that laid eggs the size of his face.

It had been five weeks since he joined the committee, but I still didn't know a single graspable detail about Prakash. He remained two-dimensional, like a sketch waiting to be filled in.

A security guard told us we could return to our offices. Our building had fifteen storeys, most of which were reserved for the FWC. There were only a handful of us standing outside. I waved to someone who looked familiar, but he didn't recognise me.

Susan refused to believe me when I told her Prakash looked a little bit different each day, as if he was not one person but an army of twins.

'You can't have an army of twins,' Susan said. 'Twins are by definition a pair. What's your problem with him? You think he's some spybot trying to steal your collection of sleep artefacts?'

'What if he's a con artist?'

'Why don't you just follow him on Instagram?'

'I don't want to look at another screen for a while. I've been plagued by migraines that make my vision blurry.'

We were at Susan's flat. A grackle landed on a tree outside the window. It struck me that Prakash's eyes were uncannily bird-like. Susan moved closer to me and offered me a head massage, which led to me trying to kiss her.

She stopped me and said, 'I like women, but women who dress up as men.'

'Are you saying I'm not butch enough for you?'

'It's more complicated than that.'

'I'm going. This is embarrassing.'

'Stop it. Do you know Emily Dickinson wrote a series of letters to an anonymous man, but it turned out they were intended for her sister-in-law.'

'That makes me feel so much better.'

I knew I was being childish, but I couldn't help myself. I slipped my feet into my sneakers without bothering to tie them, almost tripped at the door, and accidentally slammed it behind me as I left.

Artefact #113

Interpretation of Dreams by Sigmund Freud (1913). A first edition English translation of Freud's book. This particular artefact was a donation from the library of the now defunct Indian Psychoanalytical Society.

I started scattering rice grains and breadcrumbs on the window parapet at home and watched the birds that gathered in the evenings. They were usually pigeons, who spent the rest of the day fluffing their feathers while lined up along the roof of the building across from mine. Susan and I continued our weekly afternoon tea at her flat, pretending nothing had ever happened to disrupt our friendship.

The committee went on official hiatus, but we were asked to continue our individual research. Prakash's background check went through and he finally stopped bringing me confidential information about the artists and engineers whose works we procured.

During Makar Sankranti, the kite festival, Prakash came to the office with a bandaged arm. 'I got slashed while flying a kite,' he said. He turned his face to the right in order to look at me with his left eye. I wondered whether his eyes had always been that far apart.

Susan still didn't believe me. 'Now you think he's not only an army of clones but a flock of birds? I read a funny poem about birds recently. About a woman who was bored of poems with birds in them. I also don't like poems with teeth in them.' She offered me a cup of her newest concoction, which was meant to relieve stress.

'The other day I was snacking on masala peanuts when Prakash came in to ask me about our new project. I offered him some peanuts and he just leaned over and pecked at the bowl with his teeth. He blushed, pretended as if it hadn't happened and ran out.'

'Now you're just making stuff up.'

'My vision has grown pretty bad with the headaches.'

'What's the new project?'

'I don't know if you have the security clearance, so I can't tell you.' Sometimes I still wanted to hurt Susan because it established us as intimates, because I still had feelings for her, and because I wanted to experience her anger.

'Oh,' she said.

'It's just a collection of cyanotypes.'

At one of the final meetings of the committee, Susan arrived wearing leather gloves. When I asked to see her hands, she seemed startled.

'I don't need my palm read,' she said.

'Take off the gloves.'

'Why are you being weird? Are you just upset because I don't have feelings for you?'

Her words sent a jolt of energy to my sternum, but the new light had habituated me to disruptive emotional experiences. Her cruelty barely registered in my thoughts. The old metaphors no longer applied because fences, fortresses, thorny wreaths couldn't protect our symbolic hearts. The light seeped in through the epidermis, past the rib cage.

One of the scientists speculated that the new light worked as an alarm bell to amplify what we already felt. These weren't new symptoms but the old ones with the volume dialled up. I felt like the numbness had been cranked up and all other experiences were memories, which I could visualise but remained emotionally disconnected from, like conceptual art or scenes in a video game.

'Don't give me that look,' Susan said. She removed one glove by holding it between her front teeth. Her hand was covered in red blisters and a gooey white substance.

'You need a doctor to treat this. It's oozing.'

'That's the ointment I'm using. I spilled one of the glass jars and thought nothing of it. It must have got on my hands when I wiped it up.' She'd painted her nails a bright red that matched the inflamed splotches on her skin.

Eventually, the FWC was disbanded as the money ran out. A private art gallerist offered to turn our time capsule into a contemporary exhibit under the theme of dystopias. 'I thought dystopias were fictional,' Prakash said, when I told him the news on our last day.

'Everything comes true eventually,' Susan said. 'Like the monkeys on typewriters theory suggests.'

The three of us went out for drinks and I noticed how everyone at the bar looked young and had cheekbones that looked like an evolutionary adaptation of the selfie era. The new light sped up our metabolism.

'I'm happy to act as a reference for your next job,' I said to Prakash, but he laughed as though I'd delivered the punchline to a joke I wasn't in on.

We returned to the office because Susan had an urge to investigate the file cabinets. 'There must be answers,' she kept saying. 'Or at least something for an erasure poem.'

The security guard who checked our office ID cards could tell we were drunk but didn't seem to care. There were rumours that the building would be demolished and turned into a parking garage. We took the stairs to the fifth floor, not wanting to be caught on the elevator cameras. Prakash went to the utility closet and returned with a master key for the cabinets.

'It's always good to know where things are,' he said in response to our gleeful chanting of his name.

The first file cabinet was empty, and so were the next few we tried. One was filled with blank printer paper, hole punches, boxes of rubber-bands, and staple pins but no staplers. We sat down on the floor after finding nothing but empty cabinets.

'Why lock them?' I asked.

'Do you know the Wife of Bath's Tale? There's a knight who approaches twenty-four dancing women for answers, but each time he's near enough to speak, they vanish into thin air.'

'From Chaucer?' Prakash said. 'What's the moral of the story?'

'I forget where I was going with this,' Susan said. She no longer had her gloves on. We sat leaning against a wall with our legs outstretched and Prakash lay down on the floor. Susan's body language changed whenever we were in the presence of a man. She would sometimes cross her arms or hold her body up straight, almost stiffening but never awkward. Around Prakash, her body didn't react, which further convinced me that he could be more bird than man.

'You don't talk much,' Susan said to Prakash.

'I find words exhausting. I memorise sentences in order to communicate.'

'Are these memorised sentences?'

'When I get home, I'll retrieve this conversation from memory. I'll learn how you structure your language and talk to you in my head. I pick up people's accents too.'

I don't know how long we sat there hypnotised by the strangeness of the situation. Prakash seemed to have vanished in his usual manner, without saying goodbye. The scent of his sandalwood cologne still lingered. 'We should get going,' I said.

Before leaving, I walked the perimeter of the office and discovered a cluster of cubicles that I'd never noticed before. Had they appeared out of nowhere? They were vacant, like the rest of the building, except for a single black feather on the white laminated surface of an L-shaped desk.

ACKNOWLEDGEMENTS

'Drawing Lessons', Regional winner of the 2017 Commonwealth Short Story Prize, was first published online by *Granta* Magazine, 2017.

'Circus' was first published in *adda*, 2016, by Commonwealth Writers, the cultural initiative of the Commonwealth Foundation. www.addastories.org

'Notes from the Ruins' was first published in *Let's Tell the Story Properly,* Ellah Wakatama Allfrey (Ed), Dundurn Press, 2015.

'Radio Story', Regional winner of the 2012 Commonwealth Short Story Prize, was first published online by *Granta* Magazine, 2012.